Stanley N[illegible]

Story Sack.

Round *and* Round *the* Garden

and other

Action Songs

This is a Parragon Book
First published in 2000

Parragon, Queen Street House, 4 Queen Street, Bath BA1 1HE, UK

Produced by The Templar Company plc,
Pippbrook Mill, London Road, Dorking, Surrey RH4 1JE, UK

Cover designed by small world creations Ltd
Compiled and edited by Caroline Repchuk
Designed by Kilnwood Graphics

Printed and bound in Indonesia
ISBN 0 75253 455 6

Round and Round the Garden

and other Action Songs

p

The Nursery Collection

Round and Round the Garden
And Other Action Songs
The Nursery Collection

Contents

Round and Round the Garden

Round and round
the garden,
Like a teddy bear.

One step, two steps,
Tickly under there!

Round and round
the haystack,
Went the little mouse.

One step, two steps,
In this little house.

Circle palm

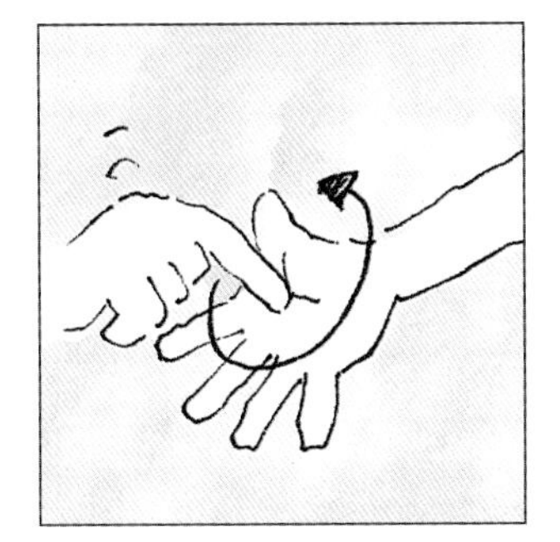

ROUND AND ROUND

Walk fingers up arm

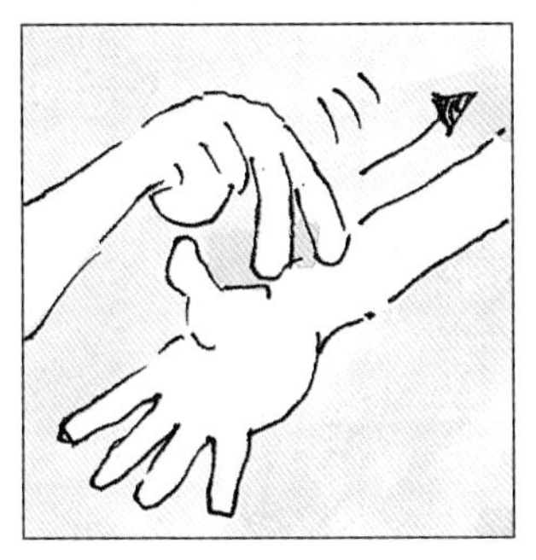

ONE STEP, TWO STEPS

Tickle!

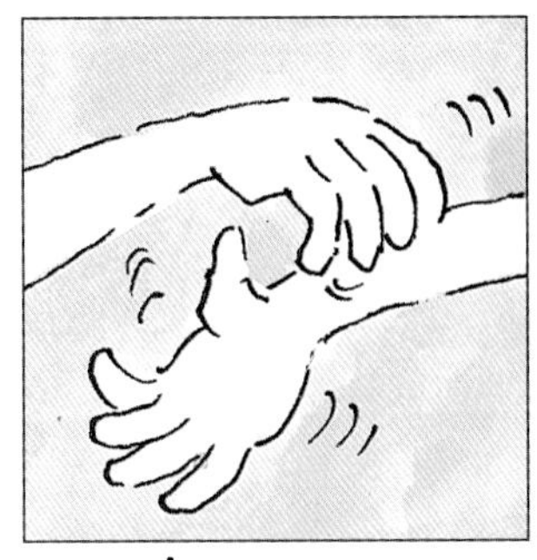

TICKLE!

The Wheels on the Bus

The wheels on the bus go round and round,
Round and round, round and round,
The wheels on the bus
go round and round,
All day long.

The wipers on
the bus go swish,
swish, swish, etc.

The horn on the bus
goes beep! beep! beep! etc.

Move fists in a circular motion

ROUND AND ROUND

Waggle both extended index fingers

SWISH, SWISH, SWISH

Pretend to press a horn

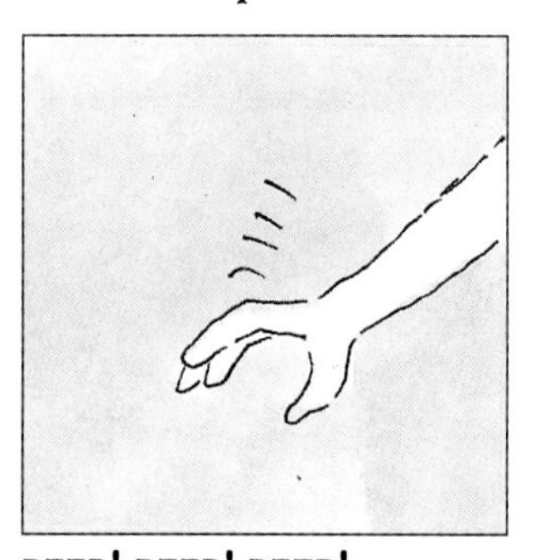

BEEP! BEEP! BEEP!

Pat thumb on rest of extended fingers

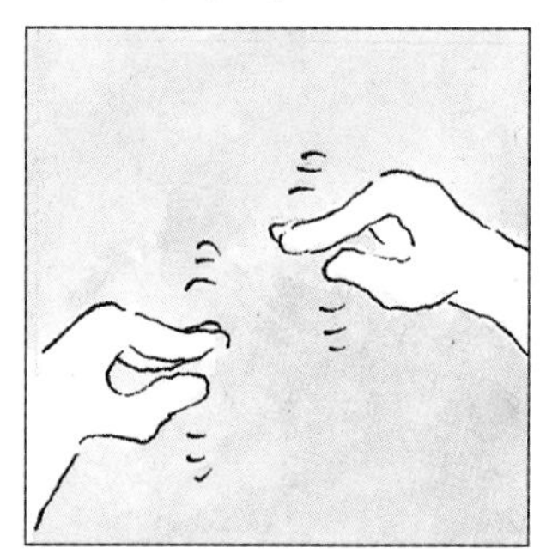

CHAT, CHAT, CHAT

The people on the bus go chat, chat, chat, etc.

The children on the bus bump up and down, etc.

The babies on
the bus go "WAAH!
WAAH! WAAH!", etc.

The grannies on
the bus go knit,
knit, knit, etc.

The wheels on
the bus go round
and round,
All day long.

Bump up and down on chair

BUMP UP AND DOWN

Make 'whaa' sound with hands around mouth

WAAH! WAAH! WAAH!

Pretend to knit with extended index fingers

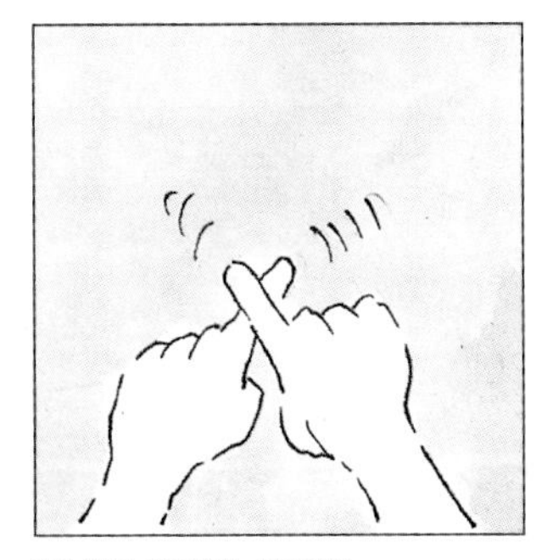

KNIT, KNIT, KNIT

Repeat first action

ROUND AND ROUND

If You're Happy and You Know It

If you're happy and you know it,
Clap your hands.
If you're happy and you know it,
Clap your hands.
If you're happy and you know it,
And you really want to show it,
If you're happy and you know it,
Clap your hands.

If you're happy and you know it,
Nod your head, etc.
If you're happy and you know it,
Stamp your feet, etc.

If you're happy and you know it,
Say "ha, ha!", etc.
If you're happy and you know it,
Do all four!

(To the tune of Frère Jacques)

I hear thunder,
I hear thunder,
Oh! don't you?
Oh! don't you?

Pitter, patter raindrops,
Pitter, patter raindrops,
I'm wet through,
I'm wet through.

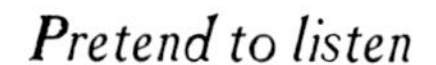

I HEAR THUNDER ...

Flutter hands like rain

PITTER, PATTER RAINDROPS

Wrap arms around body

I'M WET THROUGH

Hurry up the sunshine,
Hurry up the sunshine,
I'll soon dry,
I'll soon dry.

I see blue skies,
I see blue skies,
Way up high,
Way up high,

Point up to sky

WAY UP HIGH

Circle hands in front of chest

HURRY UP THE SUNSHINE

Pretend to shake hands dry

I'LL SOON DRY

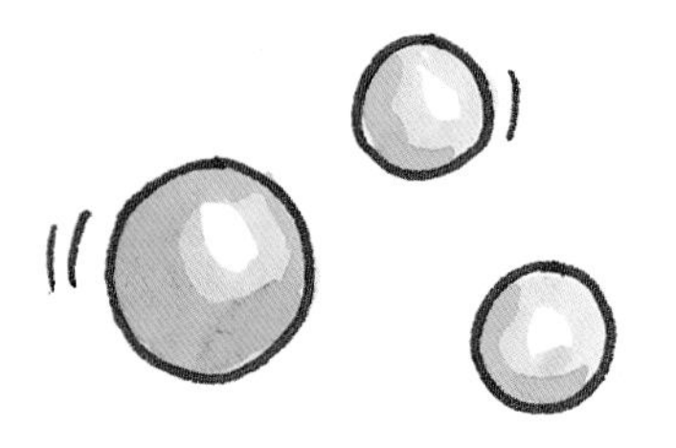

Five Little Peas

Clasp one hand round the other

Five little peas in a pea-pod pressed,

Raise thumbs, then rest of fingers

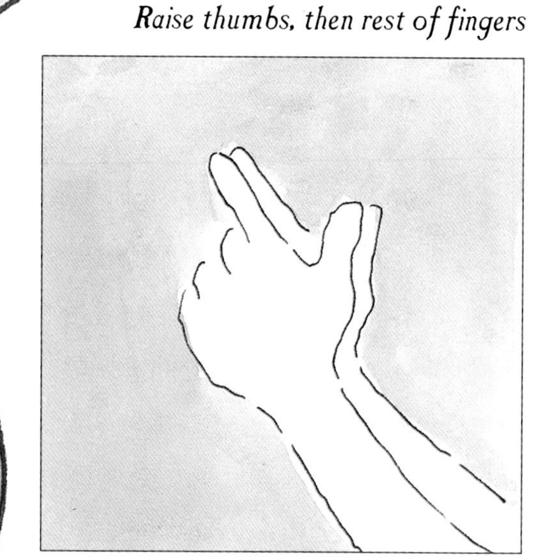

One grew, two grew, and so did all the rest.

Move hands apart slowly

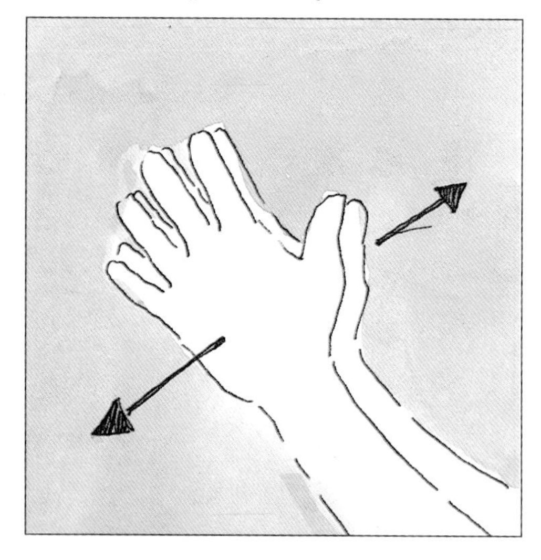

They grew, and they grew, and they did not stop,

Clap!

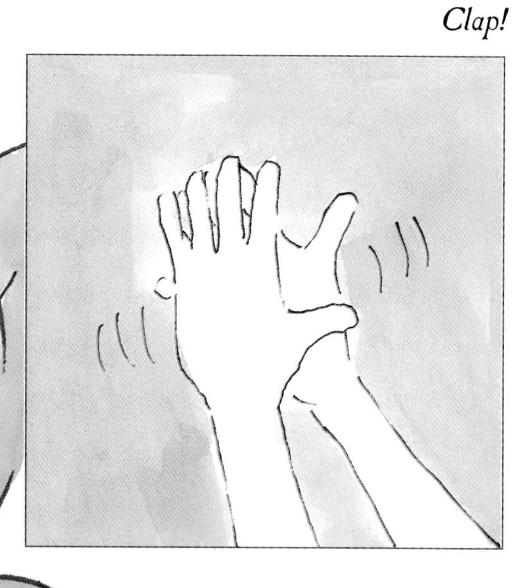

Until one day the pod went ... POP!

One Finger, One Thumb

One finger, one thumb, keep moving,
One finger, one thumb, keep moving,
One finger, one thumb, keep moving,
We'll all be merry and bright.

One finger, one thumb,
one arm, keep moving,
One finger, one thumb,
one arm, keep moving,
One finger, one thumb,
one arm, keep moving,
We'll all be merry and bright.

One finger, one thumb, one arm,
one leg, keep moving, etc

One finger, one thumb,
one arm, one leg, one nod
of the head, keep moving, etc.

This rhyme may be continued with other verses - stand up, sit down, turn around, etc.

Five Fat Sausages

Hold up five fingers

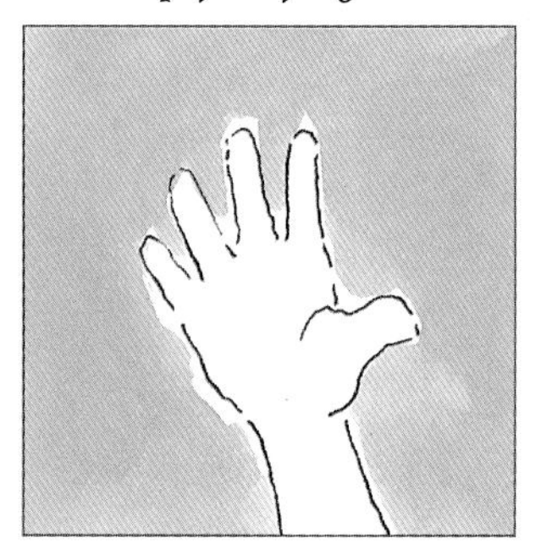

FIVE FAT SAUSAGES

Clap!

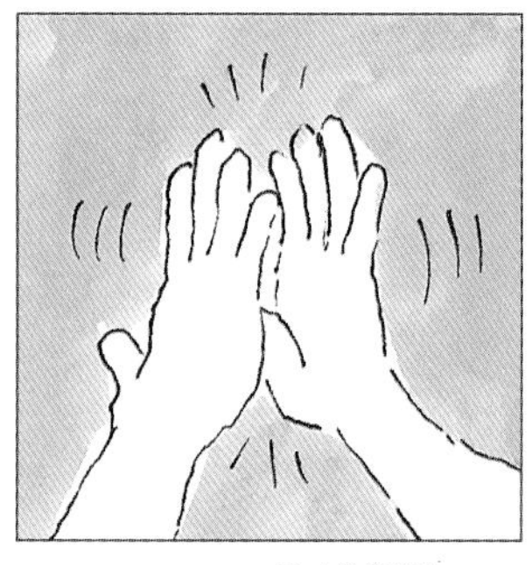

...ONE WENT BANG!

Hold up four fingers

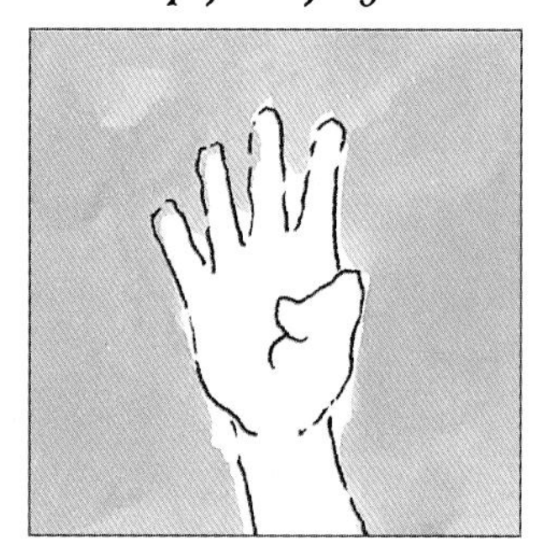

FOUR FAT SAUSAGES

Clap!

...ONE WENT BANG!

Five fat sausages frying in a pan,
All of a sudden one went 'BANG!'
Four fat sausages, etc.
Three fat sausages, etc.
Two fat sausages, etc.
One fat sausage frying in a pan,
All of a sudden it went 'BANG!'
and there were NO sausages left!

Continue until one finger left

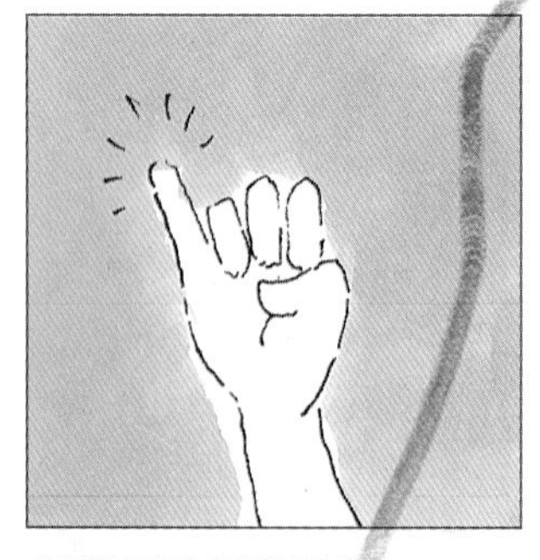

ONE FAT SAUSAGE

Clap!

...IT WENT BANG!

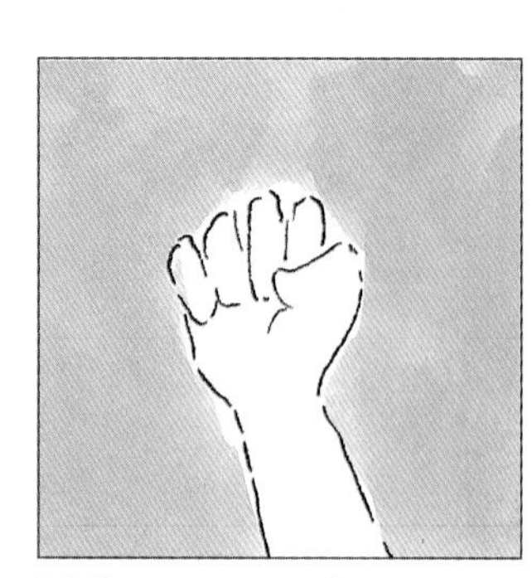

NO SAUSAGES!

Two Fat Gentlemen

Two fat gentlemen
met in a lane,
Bowed most politely,
bowed once again.
How do you do?
How do you do?
How do you do again?

Two thin ladies met in a lane, etc.
Two tall policemen met in a lane, etc.
Two little schoolboys met in a lane, etc.
Two little babies met in a lane, etc.

Repeat actions for other fingers: two thin ladies = index fingers, etc.

Hold out fists with thumbs raised

TWO FAT GENTLEMEN ...

Bend each thumb in turn

BOWED MOST POLITELY

Wiggle each thumb in turn

HOW DO YOU DO?

Wiggle thumbs together

HOW DO YOU DO AGAIN?

Ten Little Fingers

I have ten little fingers,
And they all belong to me.
I can make them do things,

Would you like to see?
I can shut them up tight,
Or open them all wide.

Hold hands up

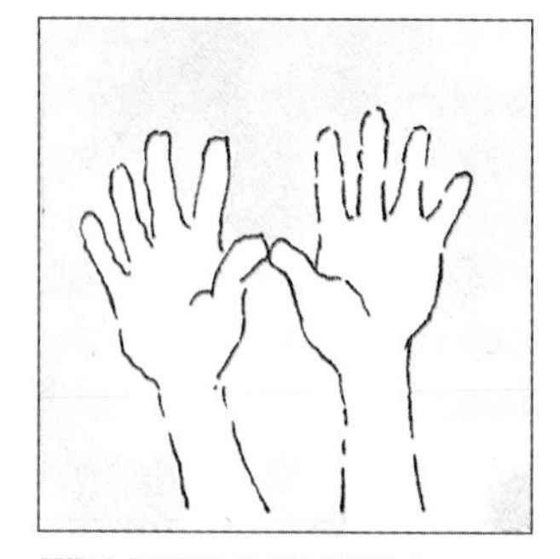

TEN LITTLE FINGERS

Waggle fingers

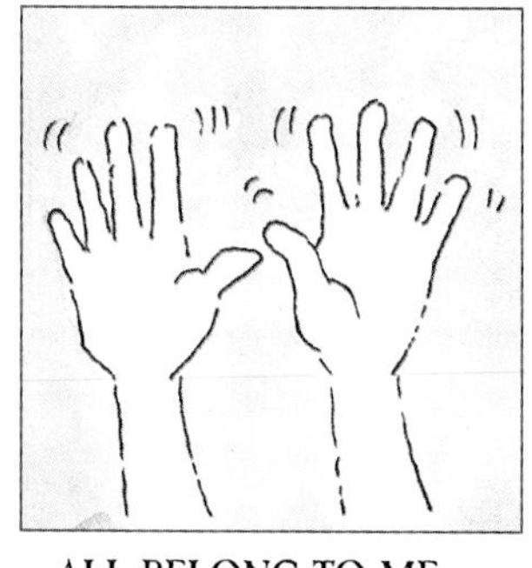

.. ALL BELONG TO ME ...

Clench fists

... SHUT THEM TIGHT ...

Open hands wide

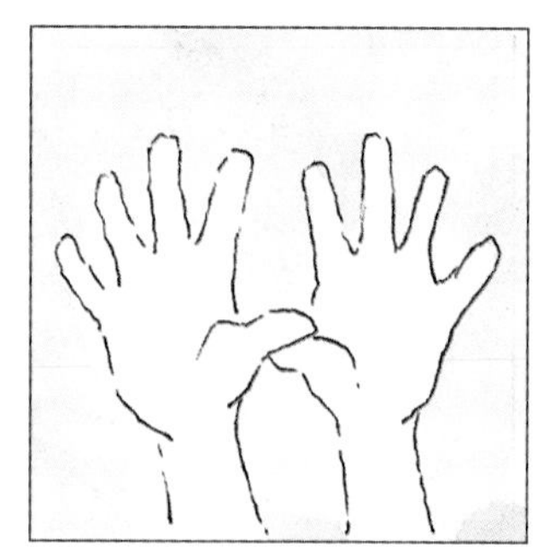

... OPEN THEM ALL WIDE

Put them all together,
Or make them all hide.
I can make them jump high;

I can make them jump low.
I can fold them quietly,
And hold them all just so.

Interlock fingers

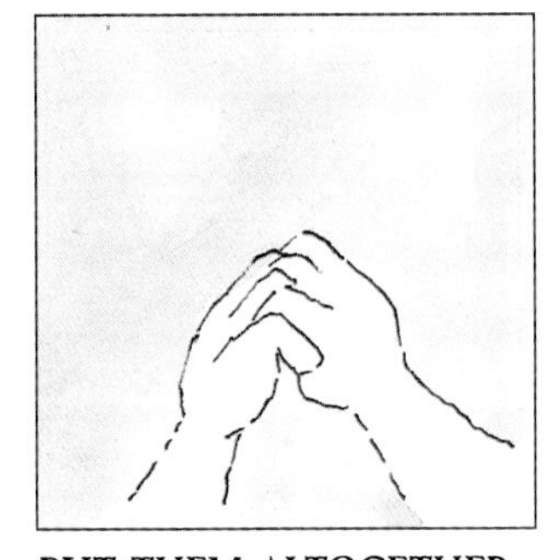

PUT THEM ALTOGETHER

Place hands behind back

... MAKE THEM ALL HIDE

Move arms up and down

...JUMP HIGH/LOW

Put hands together in lap

HOLD THEM ALL JUST SO

This Little Piggy Went To Market

This little piggy went to market,

This little piggy
stayed at home,

Wiggle ...

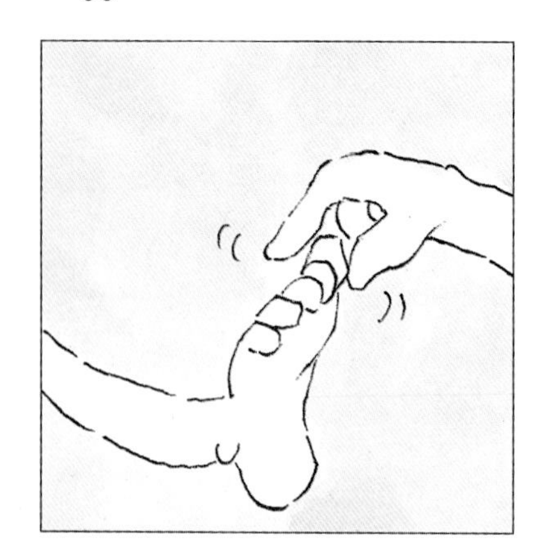

each ...

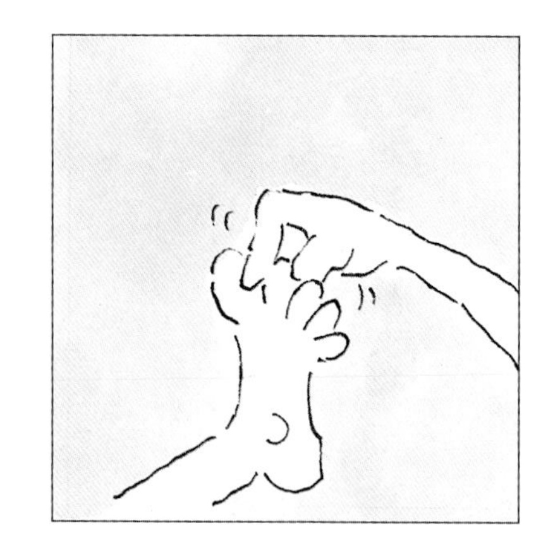

toe ...

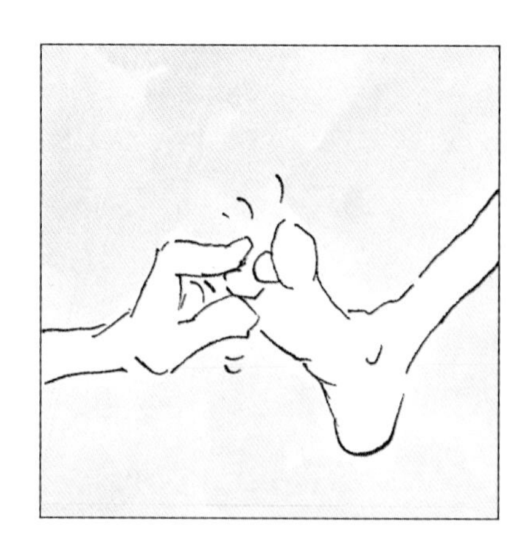

This little piggy had roast beef,

This little piggy had none,

And this little piggy cried,

"Wee-wee-wee!"

All the way home.

in ...

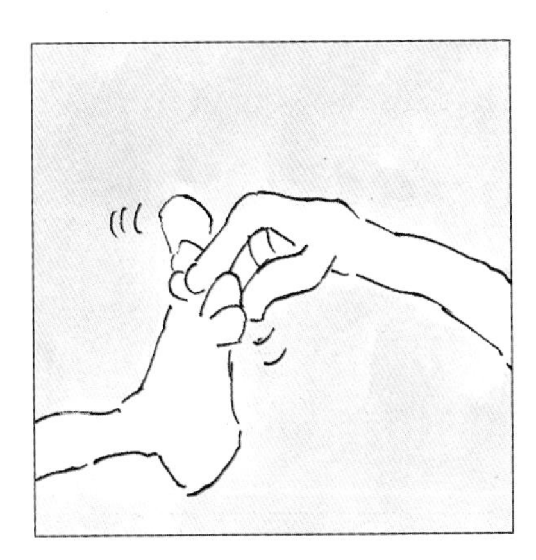

turn.

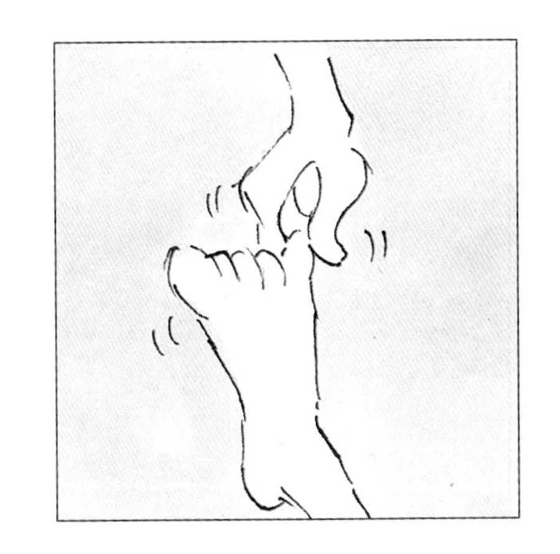

Tickle!

ALL THE WAY HOME

The Apple Tree

Here is the tree with leaves so green.
Here are the apples that hang between.
When the wind blows the apples fall.
Here is a basket to gather them all.

The Cherry Tree

Once I found a cherry stone,
I put it in the ground,
And when I came to look at it,
A tiny shoot I found.

The shoot grew up and up each day,
And soon became a tree.
I picked the rosy cherries then,
And ate them for my tea.

Make hole with one hand and pretend to plant stone

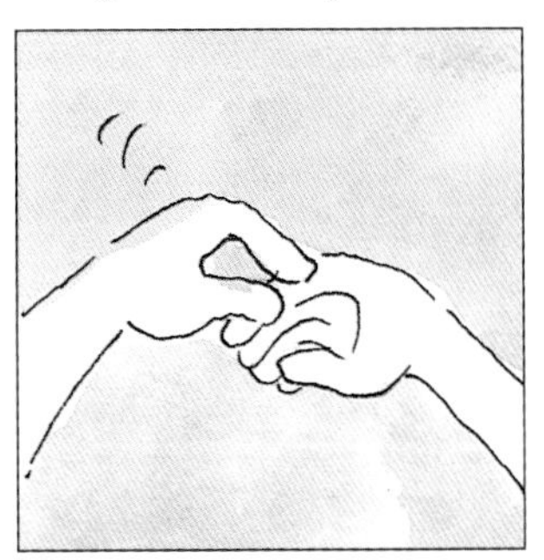

ONCE I FOUND ...

Slowly push finger up through 'hole'

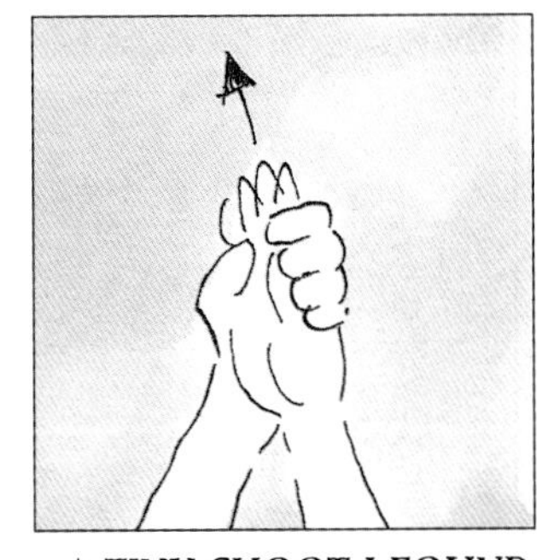

...A TINY SHOOT I FOUND

Push hand up through hole, and hold wrist

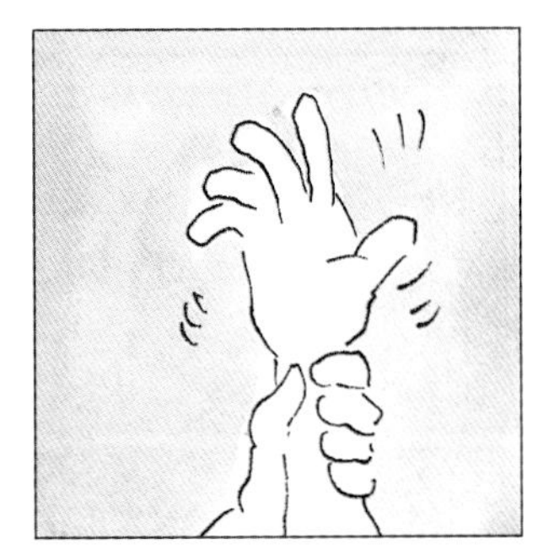

... SOON BECAME A TREE

Pretend to pick cherry from each finger and eat!

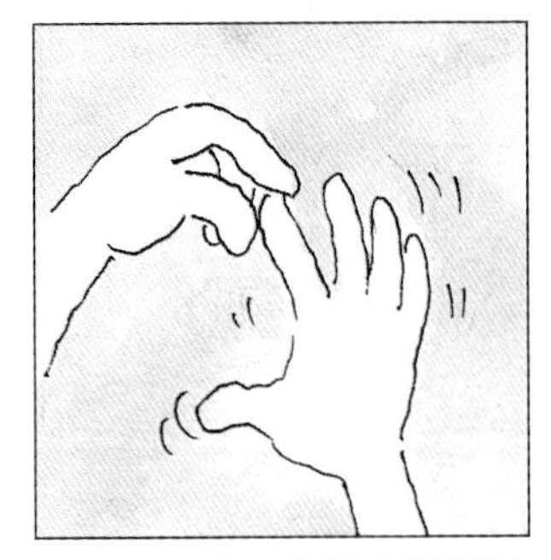

... ATE THEM FOR MY TEA

Dance, Thumbkin, Dance

Make thumbs dance

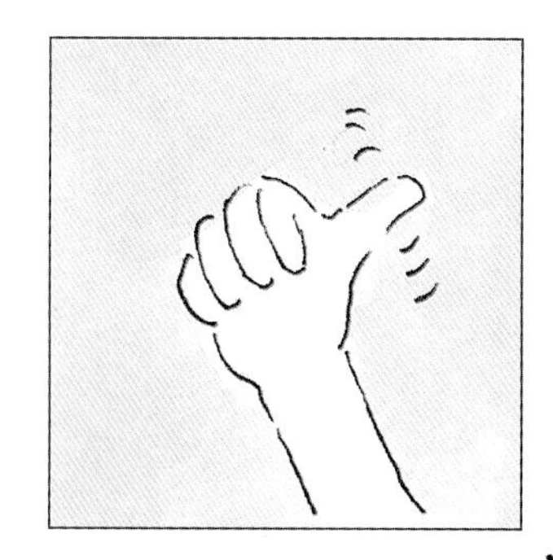

Dance, dance, thumbkin, dance.
Dance ye merrymen everyone.
Thumbkin he can dance alone,
He can dance alone.

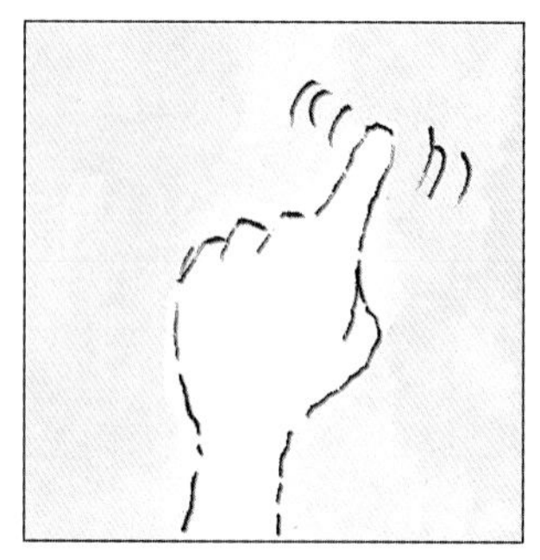

Dance, dance, foreman, dance.
Dance ye merrymen everyone.
Foreman he can dance alone,
He can dance alone.

Dance, dance, longman, dance.
Dance ye merrymen everyone.
Longman he can dance alone,
He can dance alone.

Dance, dance, ringman, dance.
Dance ye merrymen everyone.
Ringman he can dance alone,
He can dance alone.

Dance, dance, babyman, dance.
Dance ye merrymen everyone.
Babyman he can dance alone,
He can dance alone.

Ring A Ring O'Roses

Ring-a-ring o'roses,
A pocket full of posies,
A-tishoo! A-tishoo!
We all fall down!

Dance around in a ring, pretend to sneeze, then fall down on the floor

Pop Goes the Weasel

Half a pound of tu'penny rice,
Half a pound of treacle.
That's the way the money goes,
POP! goes the weasel.

A bouncing on the knee rhyme, with an extra big bounce on the "Pop!"

Here We Go Round the Mulberry Bush

Here we go round the mulberry bush,
mulberry bush, mulberry bush,
Here we go round the mulberry bush,
on a cold and frosty morning.

This is the way we brush our hair,
brush our hair, brush our hair,
This is the way we brush our hair,
on a cold and frosty morning.

Repeat chorus

This is the way we clap our hands,
clap our hands, clap our hands,
This is the way we clap our hands,
on a cold and frosty morning.

Repeat chorus

This is the way we fall on the floor,
fall on the floor, fall on the floor,
This is the way we fall on the floor,
on a cold and frosty morning.

Repeat chorus

Incy Wincy Spider

Incy Wincy spider climbing up the spout,
Down came the rain and washed the spider out.
Out came the sun, and dried up all the rain,
Incy Wincy spider climbed up the spout again.

Touch opposite index fingers and thumbs together by twisting wrists

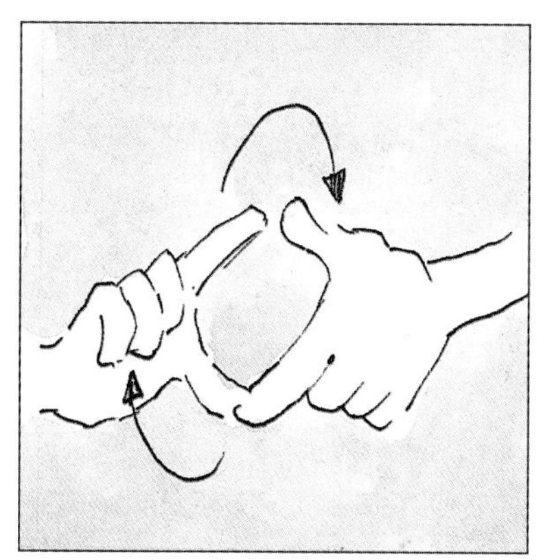

CLIMBING UP THE SPOUT...

Wiggle fingers as you lower them

DOWN CAME THE RAIN...

Make a big circle with arms. Repeat first action.

OUT CAME THE SUN...

Two Little Men in a Flying Saucer

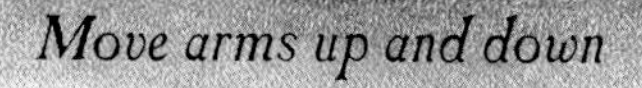
Move arms up and down

Two little men in a flying saucer
Flew round the world one day.

They looked to the left and right a bit,
And couldn't bear the sight of it,

And then they flew away.

Lift baby in circle

Turn head left

Turn head right

Cover eyes

Repeat first action

Raise arms above head

Tall shop in
the town.

Move hands up and down

Lifts moving up
and down.

Swing forearms open and shut

Doors swinging round about.

Move fists back and forth

People moving in and out.

I'm a Little Teapot

SHORT ...

AND STOUT

HANDLE

SPOUT

I'm a little teapot
short and stout,
Here's my handle,
here's my spout,
When I get my
steam up hear me shout,
Tip me up
and pour me out.

STEAM UP

SHOUT

TIP

POUR

Okey Cokey

You put your left arm in, your left arm out,
In, out, in, out, you shake it all about,
You do the okey cokey, and you turn around,
And that's what it's all about.

LEFT ARM IN...

Oh, the okey cokey,
Oh, the okey cokey,
Oh, the okey cokey,
Knees bend, arms stretch,
Ra, ra, ra!

Rhyme continues with right arm, left leg, right leg, whole self.

LEFT ARM OUT...

SHAKE IT ALL ABOUT...

TURN AROUND...

KNEES BEND, ARM STRETCH

Build a House with Five Bricks

Place fists on top of each other in turn

Build a house with five bricks,
One, two, three, four, five.

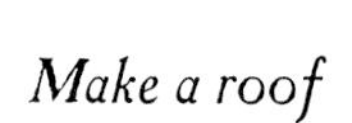

Make a roof

Put a roof on top,

Raise arms for chimney

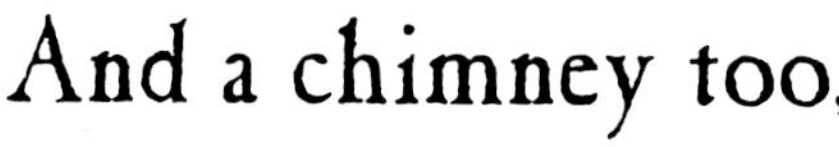

And a chimney too,

Blow!

Where the wind blows through!

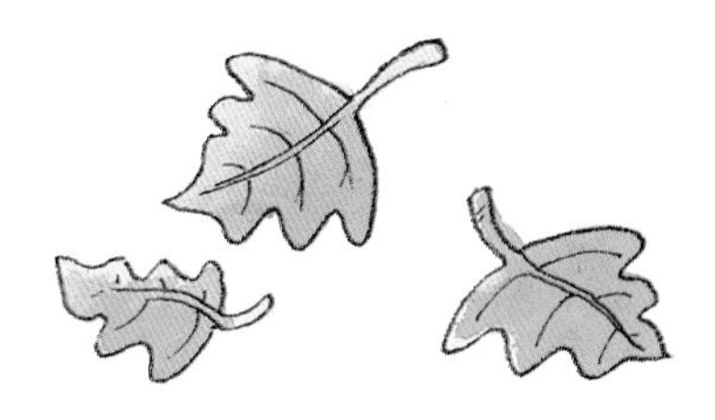

Knock at the Door

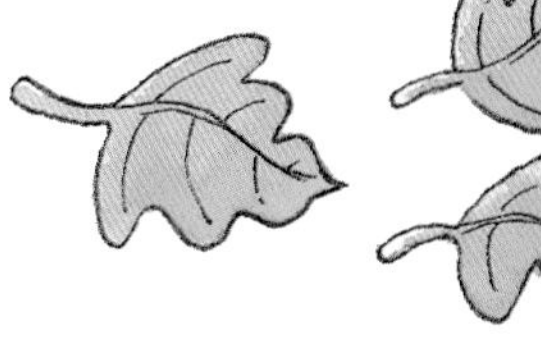
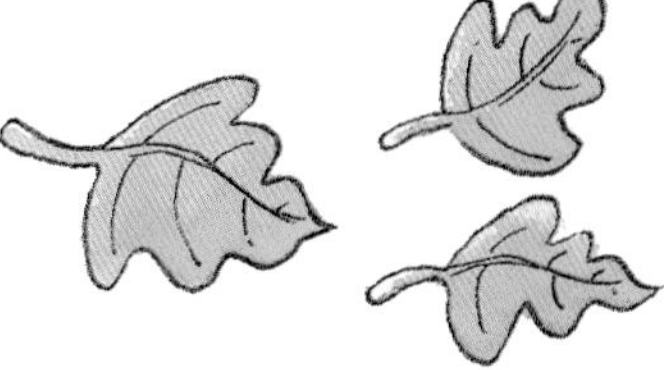

Knock on forehead

Knock at the door,

Lift eyebrow

Peep in,

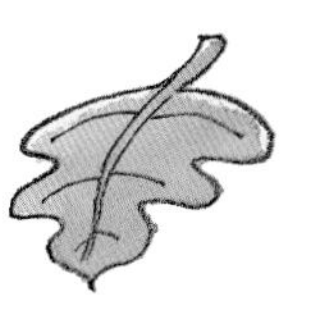

Pull ear

Ring the bell,

Push nose up

Lift the latch,

Put finger in mouth

And walk in.

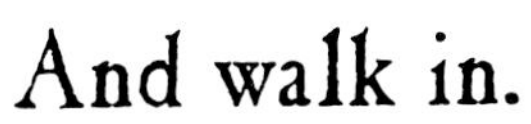

I Am the Music Man

LEADER: I am a music man,
I come from far away,
And I can play.
ALL: What can you play?
LEADER: I play piano.
ALL: Pia, pia, piano, piano, piano,
Pia, pia, piano, pia, piano.

LEADER: I am a music man,
I come from far away,
And I can play.
ALL: What can you play?
LEADER: I play the big drum.
ALL: Boomdi, boomdi, boomdi boom,
Boomdi boom, boomdi boom,
Boomdi, boomdi, boomdi boom,
Boomdi, boomdi boom.
Pia, pia, piano, piano, piano,
Pia, pia, piano, pia, piano.

LEADER: I am a music man,
I come from far away,
And I can play.
ALL: What can you play?
LEADER: I play the trumpet.
ALL: Tooti, tooti, tooti, toot,
Tooti, toot, tooti, toot,
Tooti, tooti, tooti, toot,
Tooti, tooti, toot.
Boomdi, boomdi, boomdi boom,
Boomdi boom, boomdi boom,
Boomdi, boomdi, boomdi boom,
Boomdi, boomdi boom.
Pia, pia, piano, piano, piano,
Pia, pia, piano, pia, piano.

Pretend to play each instrument in turn

Turn Around

Turn around and touch the ground,
Turn around and touch the ground,
Turn around and touch the ground,
And fall right down.

The Baby in the Cradle

The baby in the cradle
Goes rock-a-rock-a-rock.

The clock on the dresser
Goes tick-a-tick-a-tock.

The rain on the window
Goes tap-a-tap-a-tap,

But here comes the sun,
So we clap-a-clap-a-clap!

Rock arms

ROCK

Swing arm side to side

TICK-TOCK

Tap finger on hand

TAP-A-TAP

Clap!

CLAP

My Hands

My hands upon my head I place,
On my shoulders, on my face;
On my hips I place them so,
Then bend down to touch my toe.

Place hands on head

... on shoulders

... on face

... on hips

Now I raise them up so high,
Make my fingers fairly fly,
Now I clap them, one, two, three.
Then I fold them silently.

Touch toes

Raise hands in the air

Clap hands three times

Fold arms

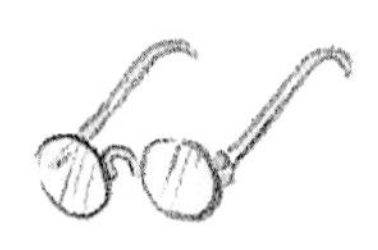

These Are Grandma's Glasses

These are Grandma's glasses,
This is Grandma's hat;
Grandma claps her hands like this,
And rests them in her lap.

Make rings round eyes

Mime hat with hands

Clap hands

Place hands in lap

These are Grandpa's glasses,
This is Grandpa's hat;
Grandpa folds his arms like this,
And has a little nap.

Make rings round eyes

Mime hat with hands

Fold arms

Pretend to sleep

Mousie

Make a fist and push other index finger in

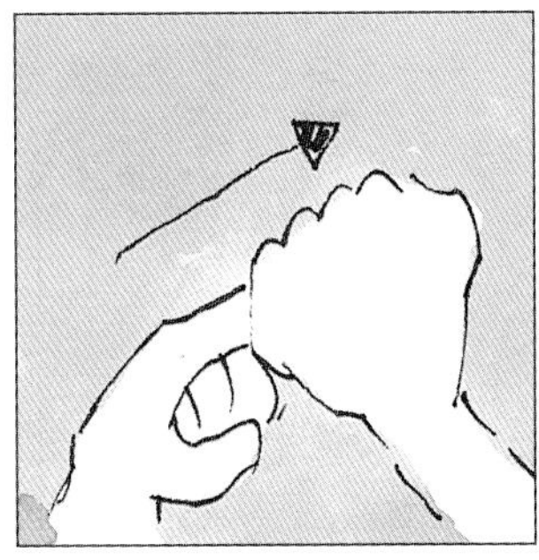

MOUSIE CREEPING

Push finger through until end appears

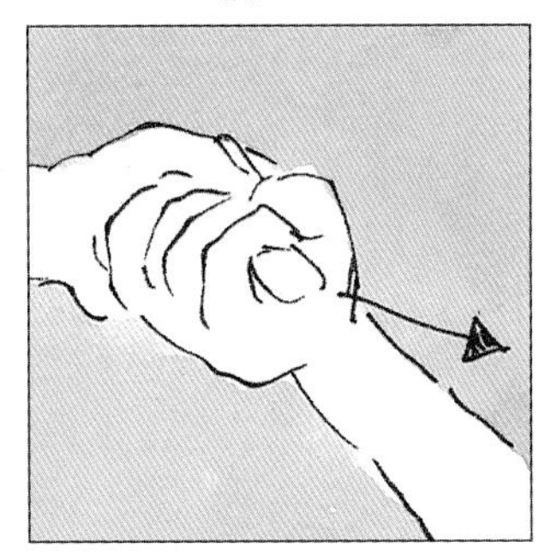

MOUSIE PEEPING

Wiggle finger

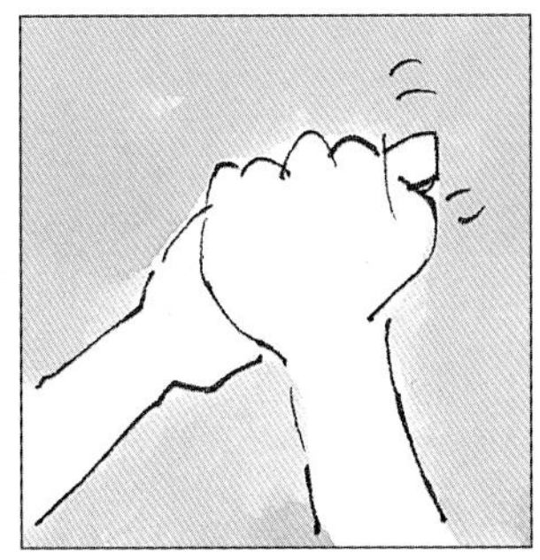

I'D LIKE TO STAY ...

Pull finger back suddenly and hide!

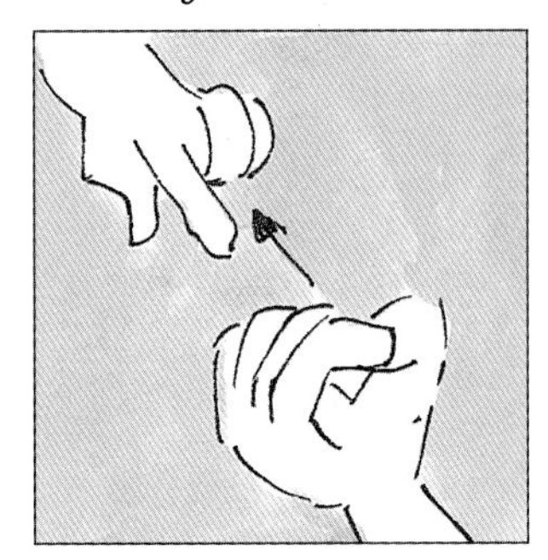

.. POPPED INTO HOLE

Mousie comes a-creeping, creeping.
Mousie comes a-peeping, peeping.
Mousie says, "I'd like to stay,
But I haven't time today."
Mousie pops into his hole
And says, "ACHOO!
I've caught a cold!"

I Saw a Slippery, Slithery Snake

I saw a slippery, slithery snake
Slide through the grasses,
Making them shake.

Weave hands side to side

Circle eyes

He looked at me with his
beady eye.

Go away!

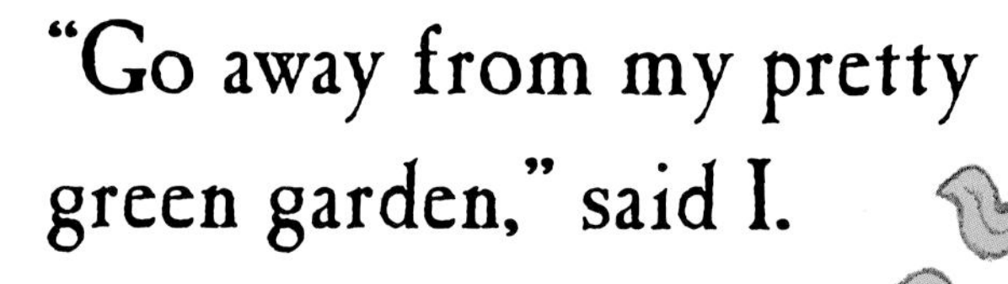

"Go away from my pretty
green garden," said I.

Repeat first action

"**Sssss**," said the
slippery, slithery snake,
As he slid through the grasses,
Making them shake.

Foxy's Hole

Put your finger in
Foxy's hole.
Foxy's not at home.
Foxy's out at the
back door
A-picking at a bone.

Interlock fingers leaving a hole between middle and ring finger

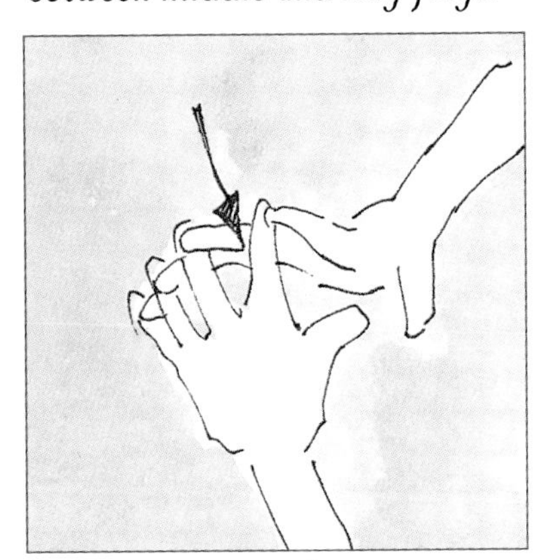

... FINGER IN FOXY'S HOLE

Get child to put finger in hole

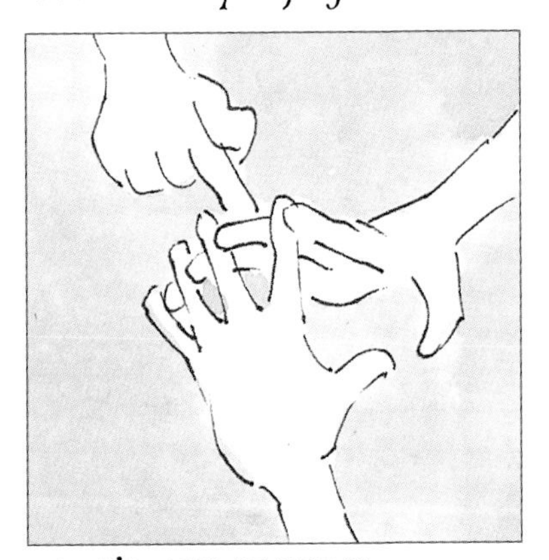

FOXY'S NOT AT HOME

Nip child's finger with thumbs

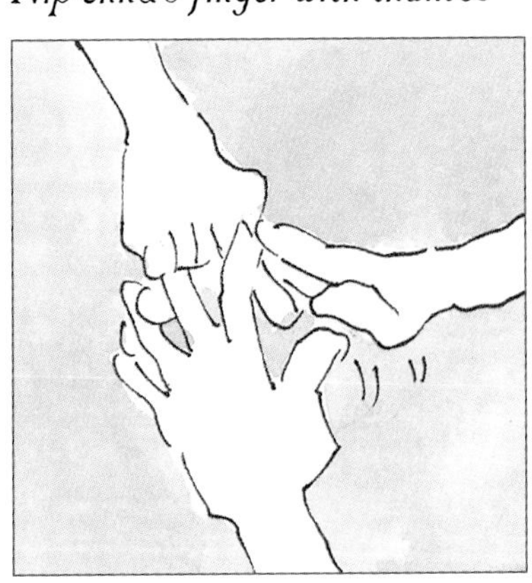

A-PICKING AT A BONE

The Beehive

Here is the beehive.
Where are the bees?
Hidden away where nobody sees.
Soon they come
creeping out of the hive,
One, two, three, four, five!

Fold one hand over the other to make hive

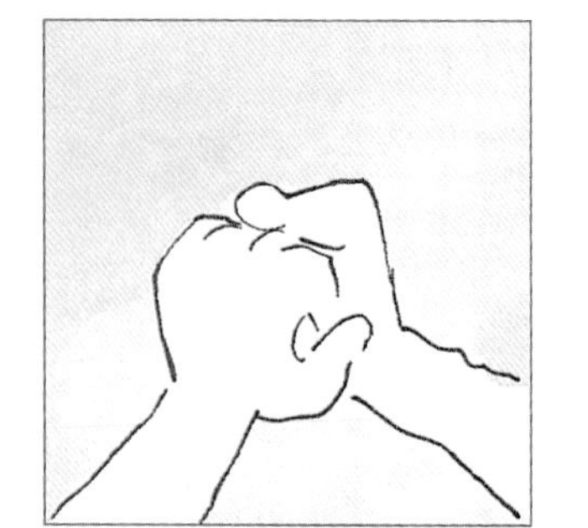

BEEHIVE

Slowly bring out thumb ..

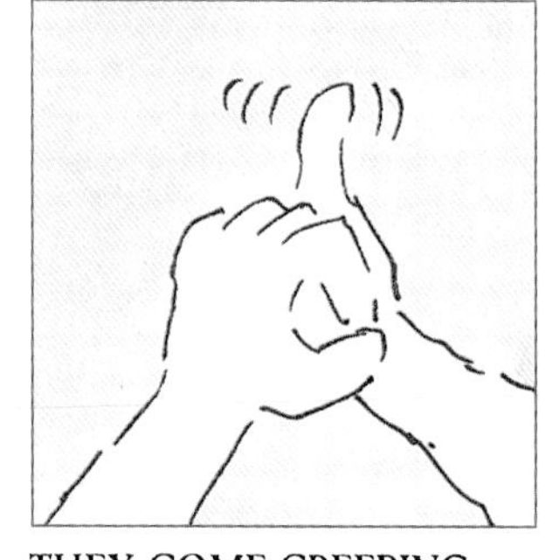

THEY COME CREEPING ...

... followed by the other fingers, one by one

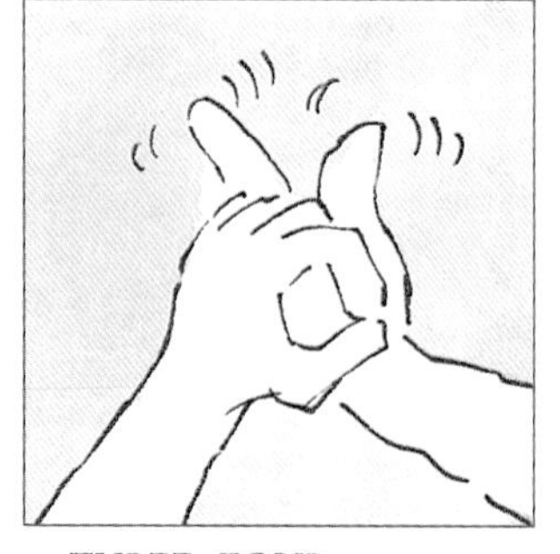

... THREE, FOUR ...

Suddenly tickle child!

...FIVE!

With My Hands on Myself

With my hands on myself,
what have we here?
This is my brainbox,
nothing to fear.
Brainbox and wibbly
wobbly woos,
That's what they taught me
when I went to school.

With my hands on myself,
what have we here?
These are my eye-peepers,
nothing to fear.
Eye-peepers, brainbox
and wibbly wobbly woos,
That's what they taught me
when I went to school.

With my hands on myself,
what have we here?
This is my nose-wiper,
nothing to fear.
Nose-wiper, eye-peepers,
brainbox and wibbly
wobbly woos,
That's what they taught me
when I went to school.

With my hands on myself,
what have we here?
This is my chest-protector,
nothing to fear.
Chest-protector, nose-wiper,
eye-peepers, brainbox and
wibbly wobbly woos,
That's what they taught me
when I went to school.

Wibbly woobly woos are the ear lobes, which should be wiggled whenever they are mentioned. Additional verses could include bread basket (tummy), knee knockers (knees), and shoe stuffers (feet).

Little Cottage in the Wood

Make roof with hands

LITTLE COTTAGE

Look through hands

MAN BY THE WINDOW

Hold up fingers

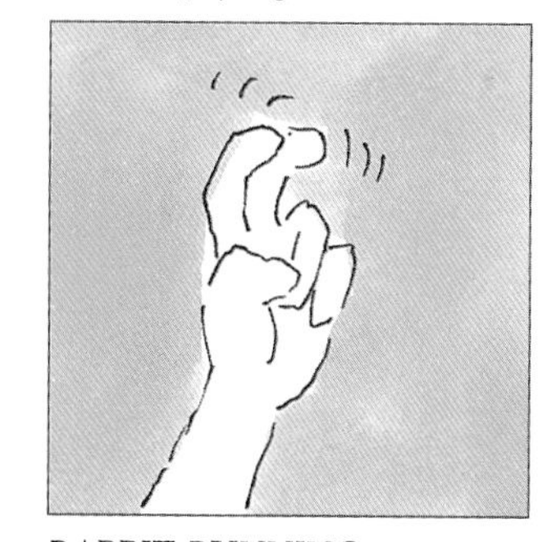

RABBIT RUNNING

Knock fist in air

KNOCKING AT DOOR

Little cottage in the wood,
Little old man by the window stood,
Saw a rabbit running by,
Knocking at the door.
"Help me! Help me! Help me!" he said,
"Before the huntsman shoots me dead."
"Come little rabbit, come inside,
Safe with me abide."

Wave arms up and down

HELP ME!

Point with one finger

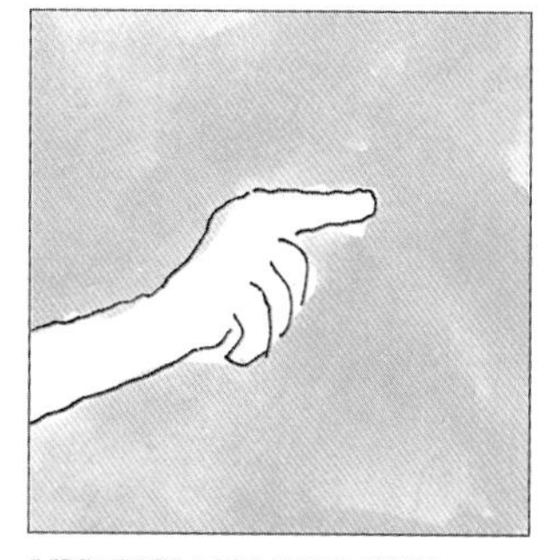

HUNTSMAN SHOOTS

Beckon with same finger

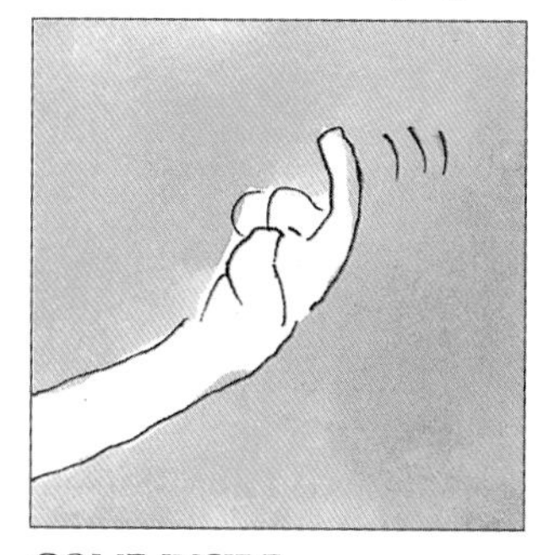

COME INSIDE

Stroke hand (rabbit)

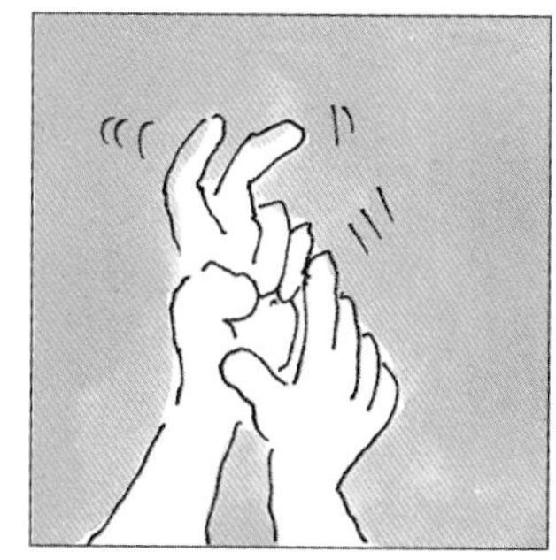

SAFE WITH ME

This is the Way the Ladies Ride

This is the way the ladies ride,
Nimble-nim, nimble-nim.

This is the way the gentlemen ride,
Gallop-a-trot, gallop-a-trot.

This is the way the farmers ride,
Hobbledy-hoy, hobbledy-hoy.

This is the way the butcher boy rides,
Tripperty-trot, tripperty-trot.

Till he falls in a ditch with a flipperty,
Flipperty, flop, flop, **FLOP!**

Bounce baby on knee, getting faster as rhyme progresses, and 'dropping' baby through knees on last verse

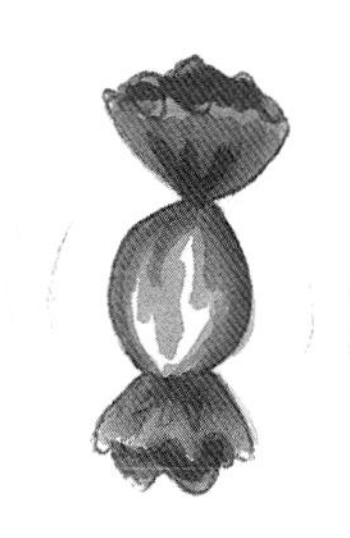

Jelly on the Plate

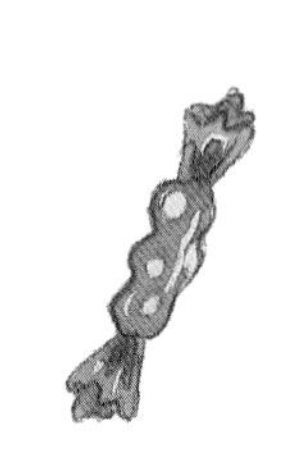

Jelly on the plate,
Jelly on the plate,
Wibble, wobble,
Wibble, wobble,
Jelly on the plate.

Rock from side to side

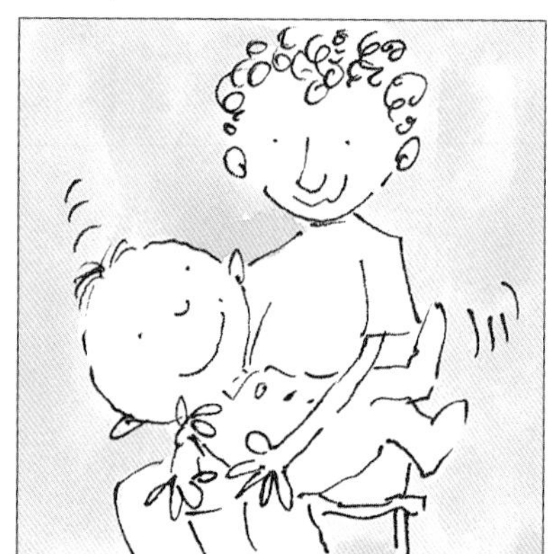

Bounce up and down

Sweeties in the jar,
Sweeties in the jar,
Shake them up,
Shake them up,
Sweeties in the jar.

Candles on the cake,
Candles on the cake,
Blow them out,
Blow them out,
Puff, PUFF, **PUFF!**

Blow!

Here's the Lady's Knives and Forks

Here's the lady's knives and forks.
Here's the lady's table.
Here's the lady's looking glass.
And here's the baby's cradle.
Rock! Rock! Rock! Rock!

Interlock fingers with backs of hands together

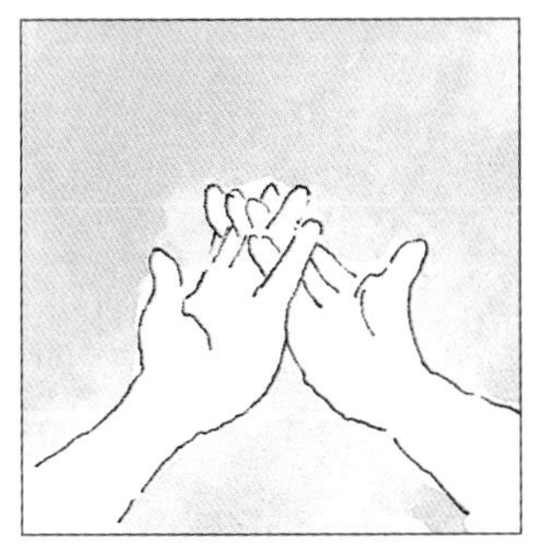

KNIVES AND FORKS...

Turn hands over and bring wrists together

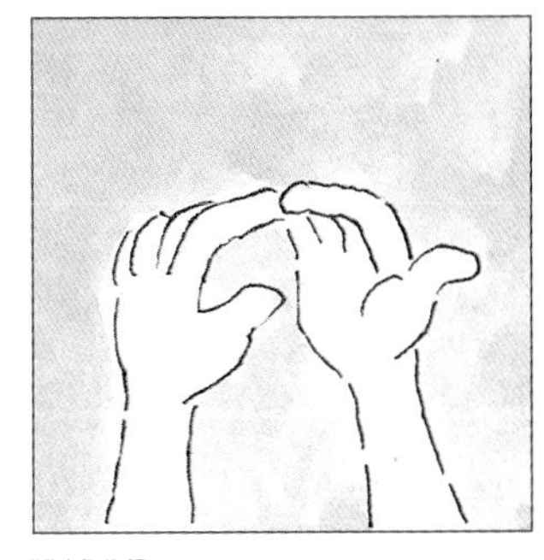

TABLE...

Raise both index fingers

LOOKING GLASS...

Raise both little fingers and rock back and forth

CRADLE - ROCK!

Gee Up, Neddy

Gee up, Neddy,
Don't you stop,
Just let your feet go
Clippety clop.
Clippety clopping,
Round and round.
Giddy up,
We're homeward bound.

Hickory Dickory Dock

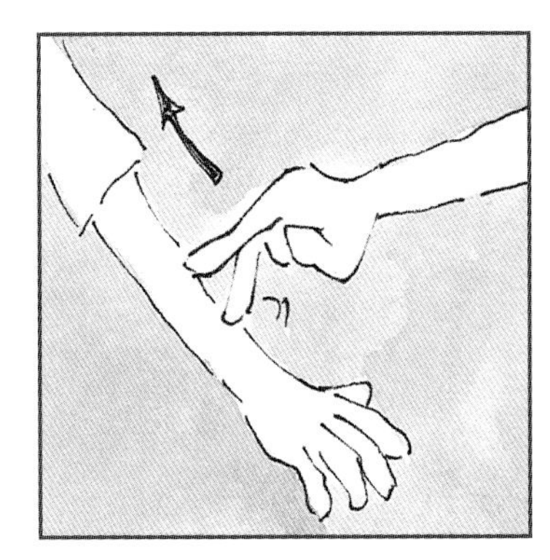

Walk fingers up arm

Hickory
dickory dock,
The mouse ran
up the clock.

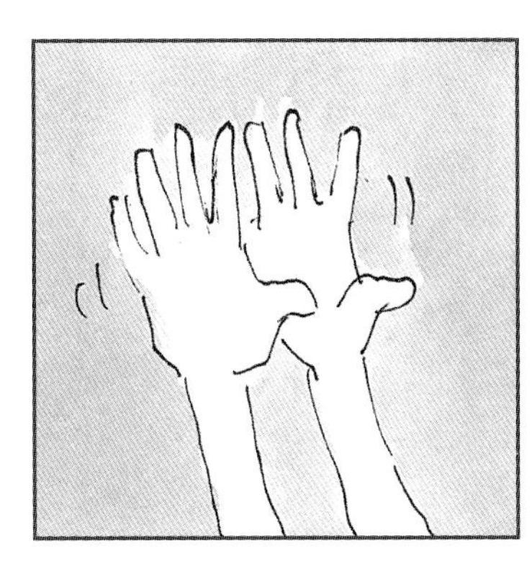

Clap once

The clock
struck one,

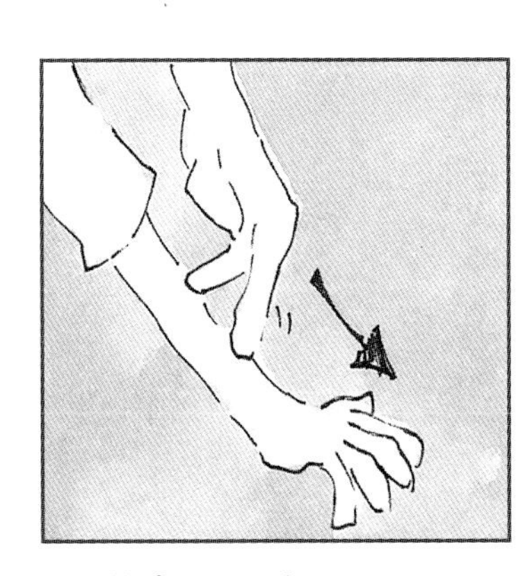

Walk fingers down arm

The mouse
ran down,
Hickory
dickory dock.

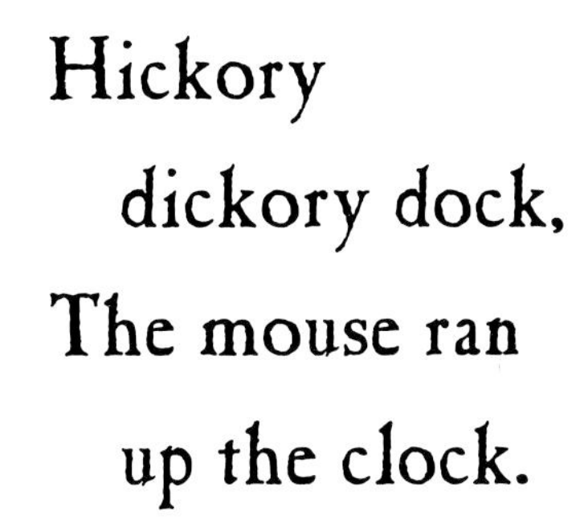

Here's a Ball for Baby

Here's a ball for baby,
Big and fat and round.

Here is baby's hammer,
See how it can pound.

Here are baby's soldiers,
Standing in a row.

Here is baby's music,
Clapping, clapping so.

Make ball with hands

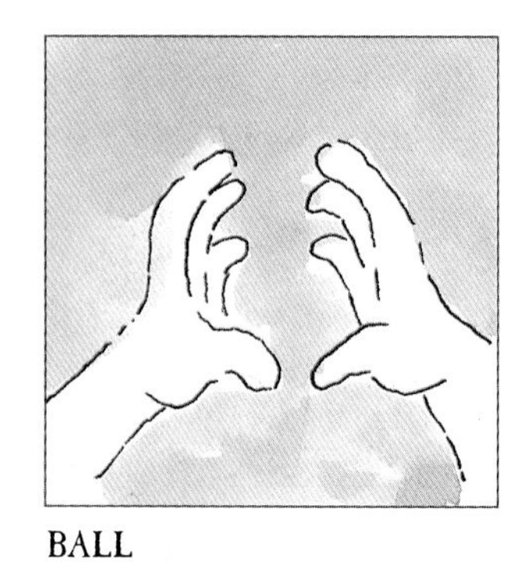

BALL

Tap fist against knee

HAMMER

Show ten fingers

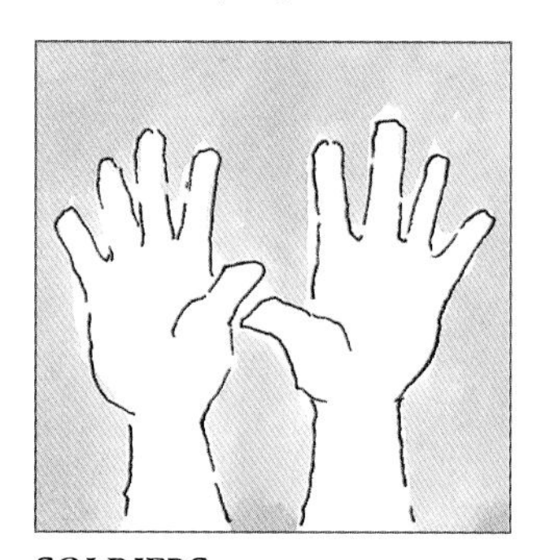

SOLDIERS

Clap hands

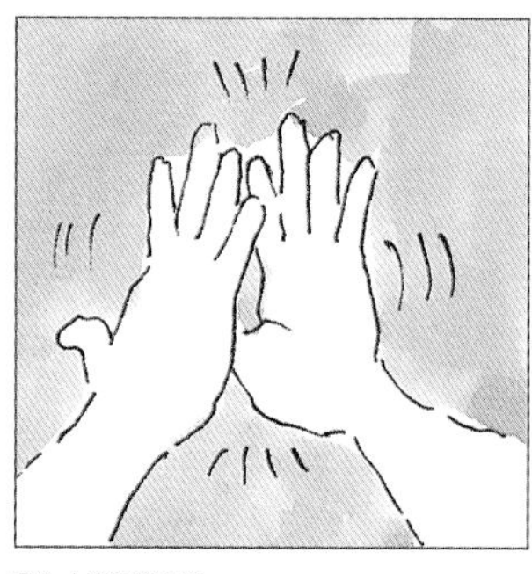

CLAPPING

Here is baby's trumpet,
TOOTLE-TOOTLE-OO!

Here's the way the baby
Plays at peek-a-boo.

Here's a big umbrella,
To keep the baby dry.

Here is baby's cradle,
Rock-a-baby-bye.

Blow through fist

TRUMPET

Hands up to eyes

PEEK-A-BOO

Pretend to hold umbrella

UMBRELLA

Rock hands in cradle

CRADLE

As Small as a Mouse

As small as a mouse,

As wide as a bridge,

As tall as a house,

As straight as a pin.

Slowly, Slowly

Slowly, slowly, very slowly
Creeps the garden snail.

Slowly, slowly, very slowly
Up the garden rail.

Quickly, quickly, very quickly
Runs the little mouse.

Quickly, quickly, very quickly
Round about the house.

Walk hand slowly up baby's tummy ...

Tickle baby during second verse

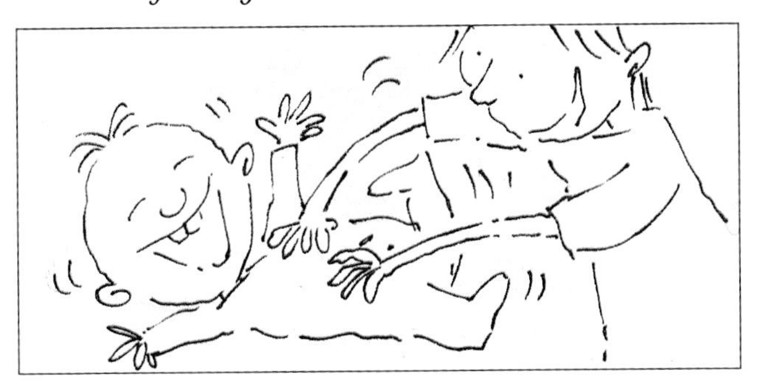

Row, Row, Row Your Boat

Row, row, row your boat,
Gently down the stream,
Merrily, merrily, merrily merrily,
Life is but a dream.

Mime rowing action throughout ...

Round About There

Round about there,
Sat a little hare,
A cat came and
chased him,
Right up there!

Circle child's palm with finger

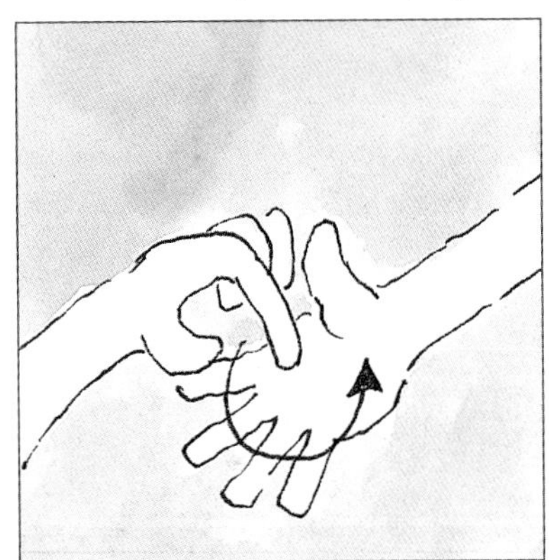

ROUND ABOUT THERE

Walk fingers up arm

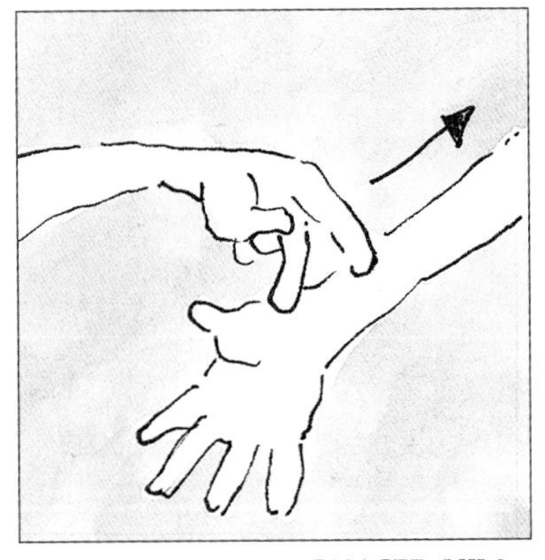

A CAT CAME AND CHASED HIM

Tickle!

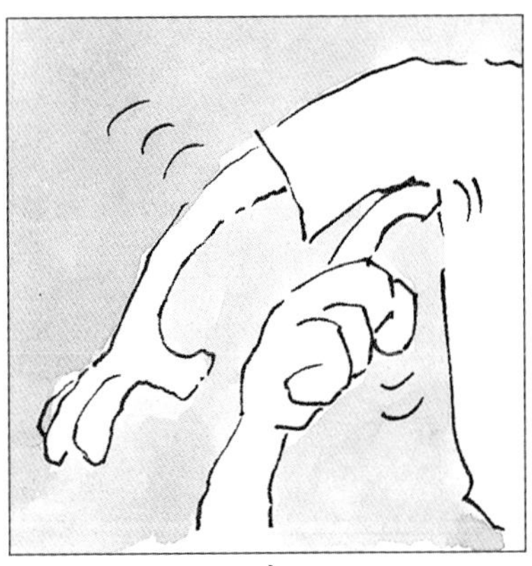

RIGHT UP THERE!

The Ostrich

Here is the ostrich
straight and tall,

Nodding his head
above us all.

Here is the hedgehog
prickly and small,

Rolling himself
into a ball.

Hold up arm

OSTRICH

Nod hand in air

NODS HIS HEAD

Interlace fingers

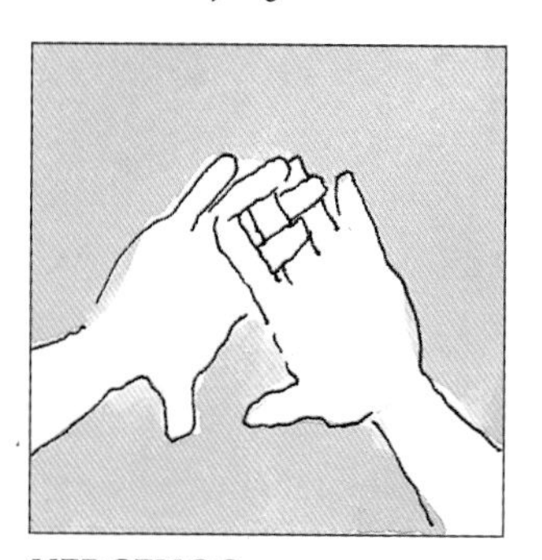

HEDGEHOG

Close hands in a ball

HEDGEHOG IN BALL

Here is the spider scuttling around,
Treading so lightly on the ground.

Here are the birds that fly so high,
Spreading their wings across the sky.

Here are the children fast asleep,
And in the night the owls do peep,

"Tuit tuwhoo, tuit tuwhoo!"

Wriggle fingers

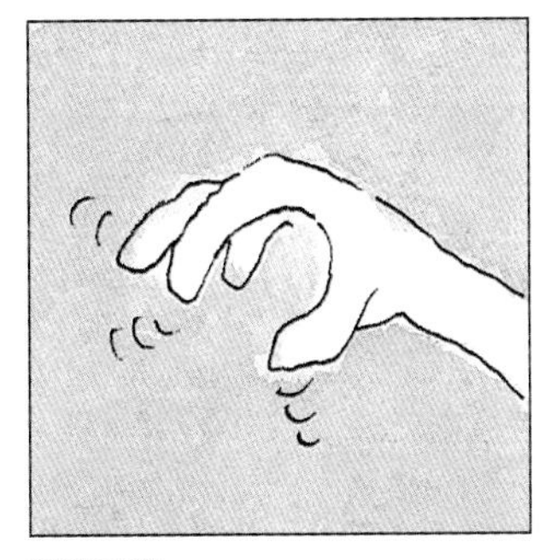

SPIDER

Lock thumbs together

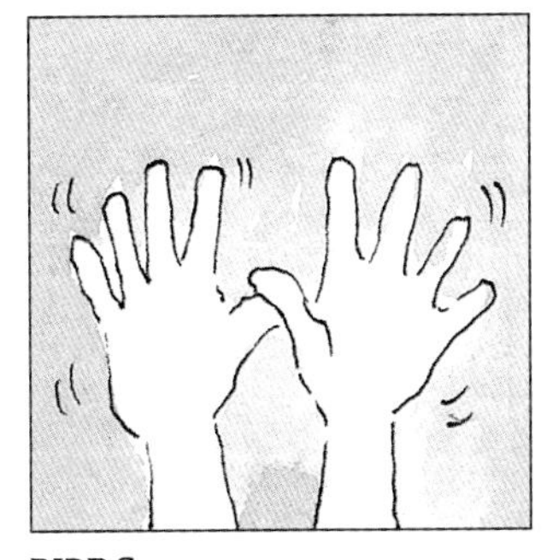

BIRDS

Pretend to sleep

CHILDREN ASLEEP

Make rings around eyes

OWLS

Five Little Soldiers

Five little soldiers standing in a row,
Three stood straight,

And two stood — so.
Along came the captain,
And what do you think?
They ALL stood straight,
As quick as a wink.

Hold five fingers up

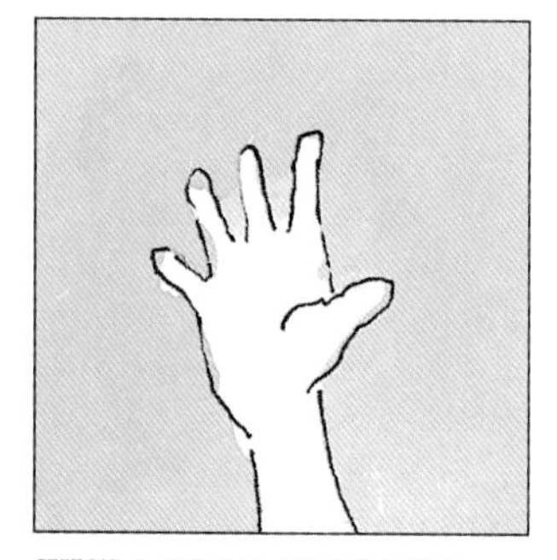

FIVE LITTLE SOLDIERS

Fold down two fingers

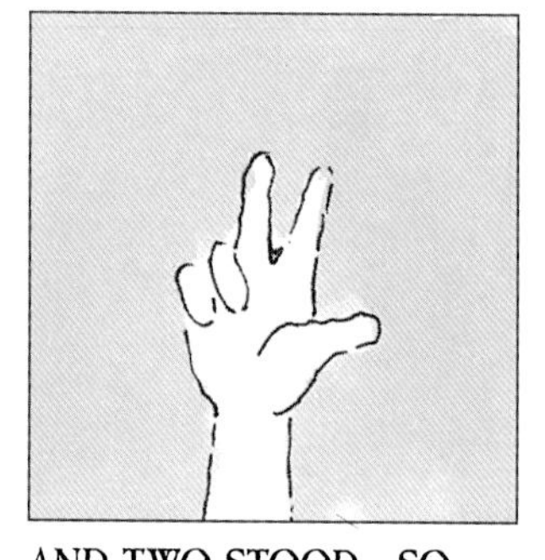

AND TWO STOOD - SO

Pass index finger of other hand in front

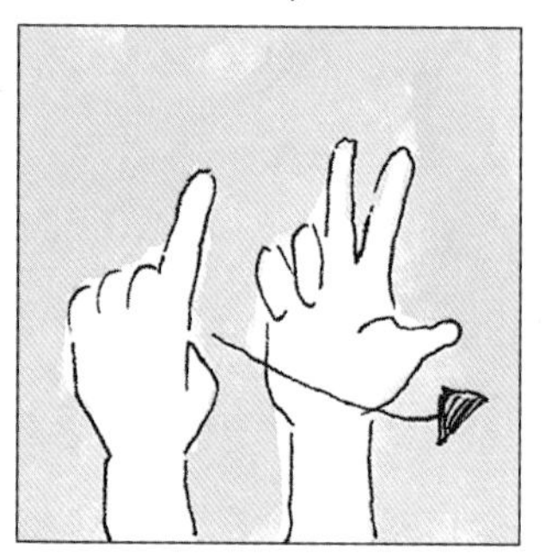

... WHAT DO YOU THINK

Straighten all fingers

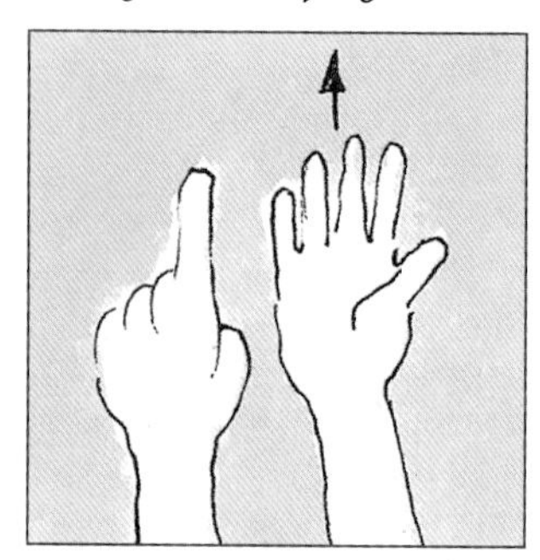

... ALL STOOD STRAIGHT

Here Sits the Lord Mayor

Here sits the Lord Mayor,

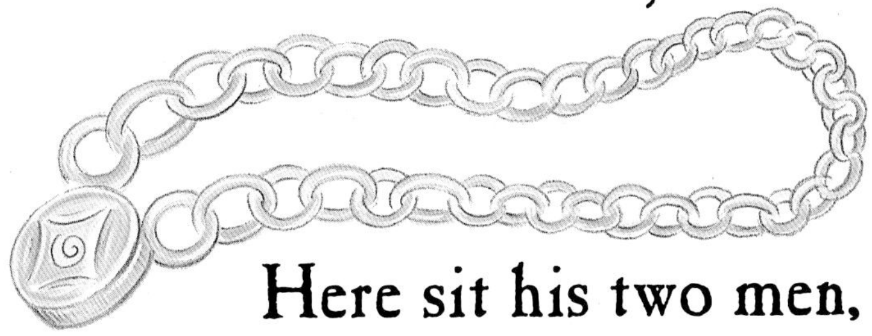

Here sit his two men,

Here sits the cocky,

Here sits the hen,

Here sit the chicks,

And here they run in,

Chin chopper,
chin chopper,
chin chopper,
chin.

Clap, Clap Hands

Clap, clap hands, one, two, three,
Put your hands upon your knees,
Lift them up high to touch the sky,
Clap, clap hands and away they fly.

Clap hands in rhythm	*Touch knees*	*Raise arms*	*Shake raised hands*

CLAP, CLAP HANDS	... YOUR KNEES	... LIFT THEM HIGH	... AWAY THEY FLY

Five Little Monkeys

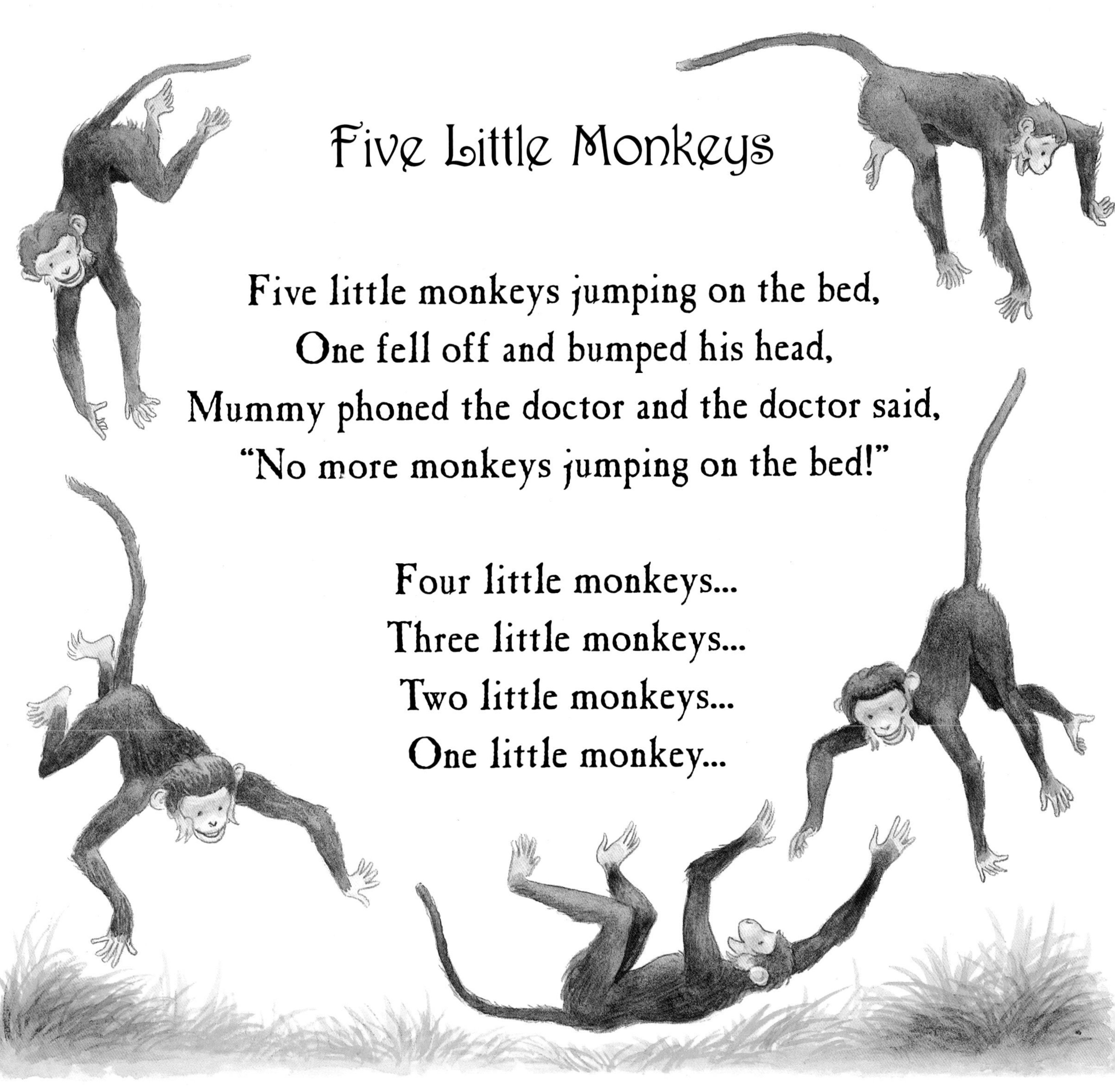

Five little monkeys jumping on the bed,
One fell off and bumped his head,
Mummy phoned the doctor and the doctor said,
"No more monkeys jumping on the bed!"

Four little monkeys...
Three little monkeys...
Two little monkeys...
One little monkey...

Repeat actions showing one less finger each time

Hold up hand

FIVE LITTLE MONKEYS

Pat top of head

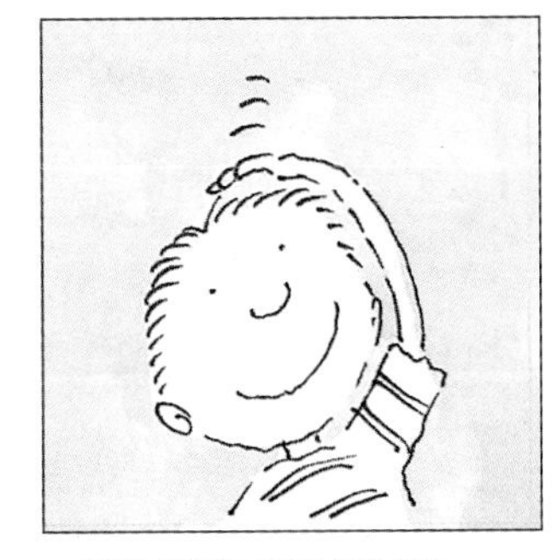

... BUMPED HIS HEAD

Pretend to hold phone

... PHONED THE DOCTOR

Waggle index finger

NO MORE MONKEYS ...

There Was a Little Turtle

There was a little turtle,
He lived in a box.
He swam in a puddle,
He climbed on the rocks.

He snapped at a mosquito,
He snapped at a flea.
He snapped at a minnow,
He snapped at me.

Cup both palms, one on top of the other

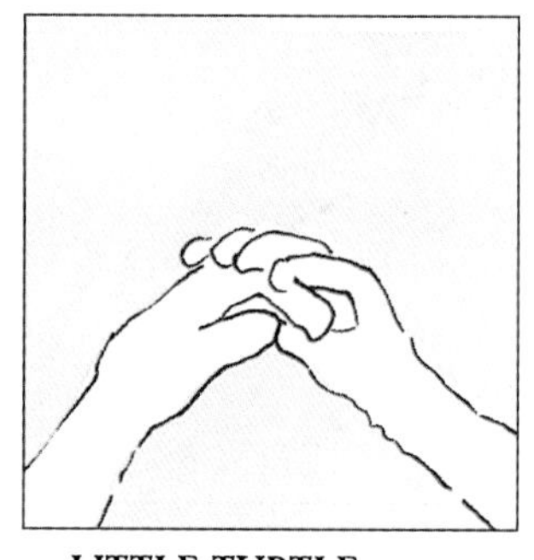

... LITTLE TURTLE

Draw a square in the air with index fingers

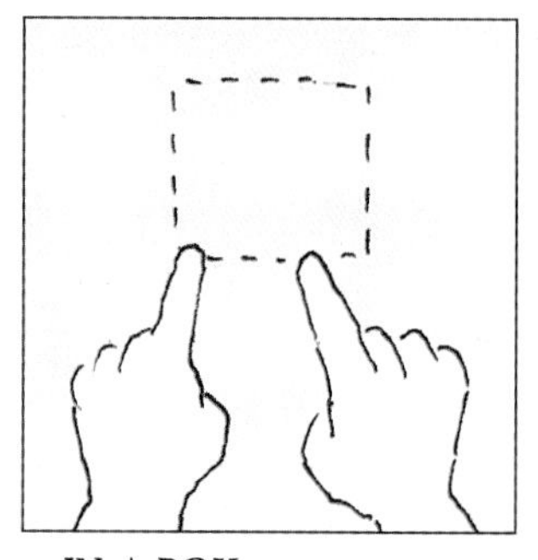

... IN A BOX

Making swimming motion with hand

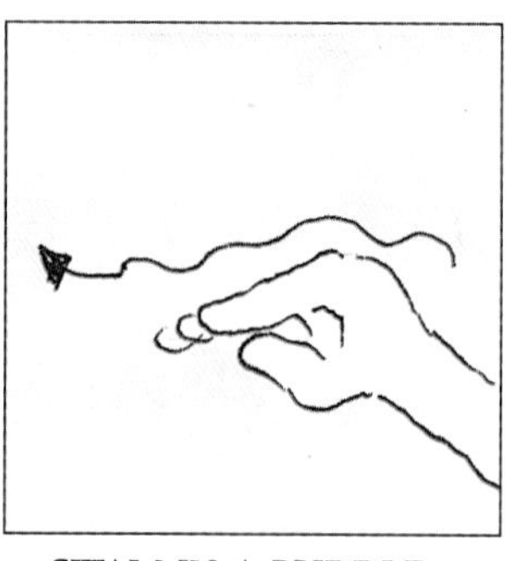

... SWAM IN A PUDDLE

Waggle all five fingers in crawling motion

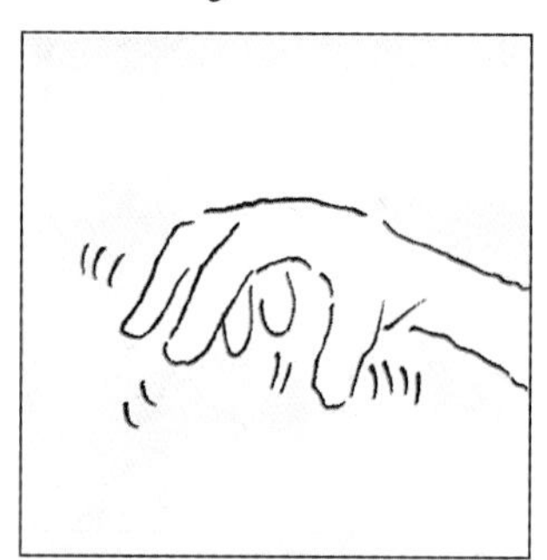

... ON THE ROCKS

He caught the mosquito,
He caught the flea.
He caught the minnow,

But... he didn't catch me!

Snap thumb and fingers together four times

HE SNAPPED ...

Clap hands together three times

HE CAUGHT ...

Shake head and point to chin

... DIDN'T CATCH ME!

The Little Bird

This little bird flaps its wings,
Flaps its wings, flaps its wings,
This little bird flaps its wings,
And flies away in the morning!

Link thumbs and flap fingers

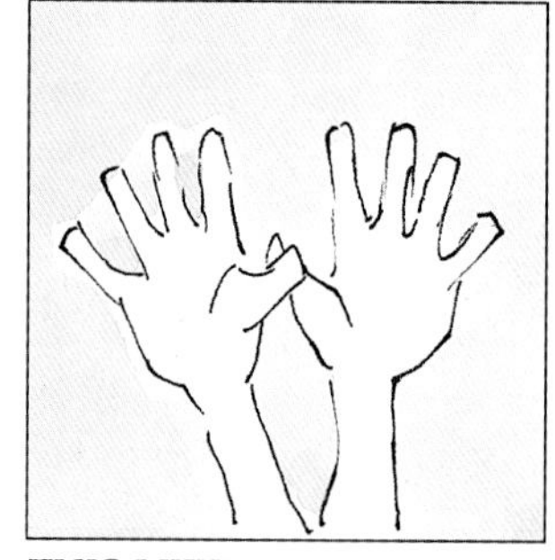

THIS LITTLE BIRD ...

Lift hands ...

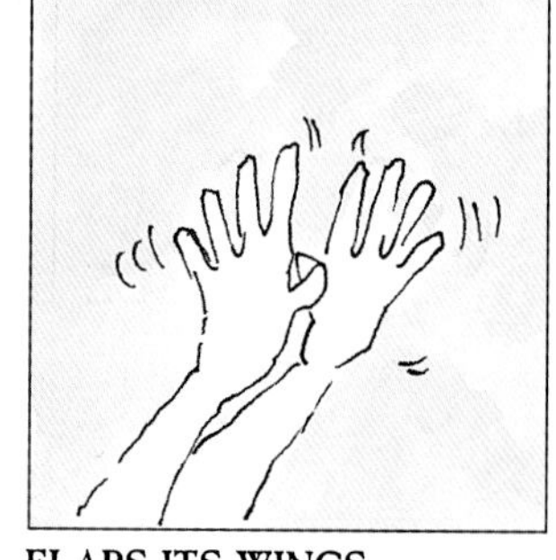

FLAPS ITS WINGS ...

still flapping ...

FLAPS ITS WINGS ...

as high as you can

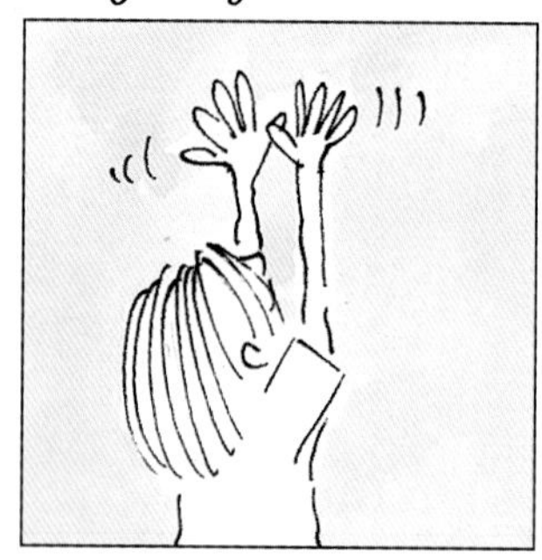

FLIES AWAY ...

Two Little Dicky Birds

Stick paper on each index finger

Hold out fingers and shake in turn

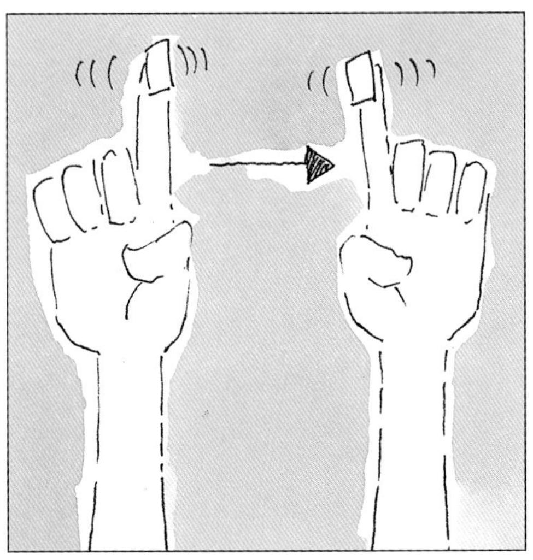

Two little dicky birds
Sitting on a wall,

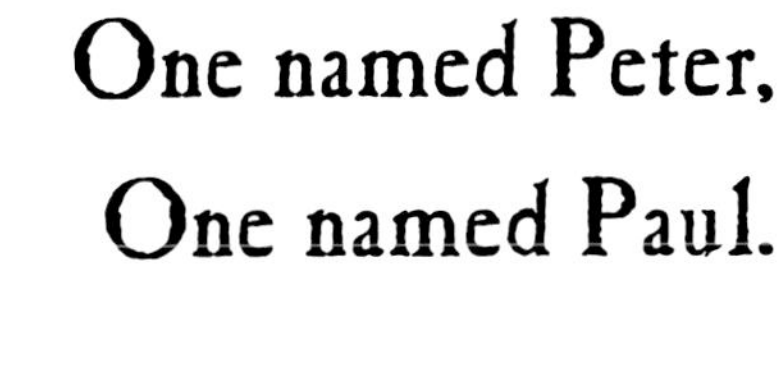

One named Peter,
One named Paul.

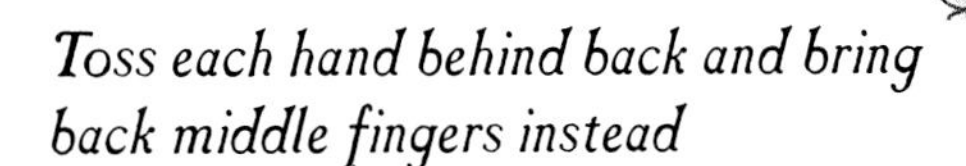

Toss each hand behind back and bring back middle fingers instead

Toss each hand behind back and bring back index fingers

Fly away Peter!
Fly away Paul!

Come back Peter,
Come back Paul.

Ten Little Men

Ten little men standing straight,
Ten little men open the gate,
Ten little men all in a ring,

Hold up ten fingers

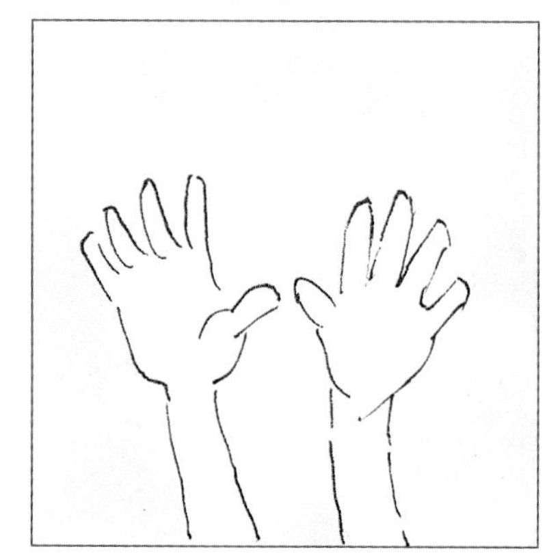

TEN LITTLE MEN ...

Turn wrists

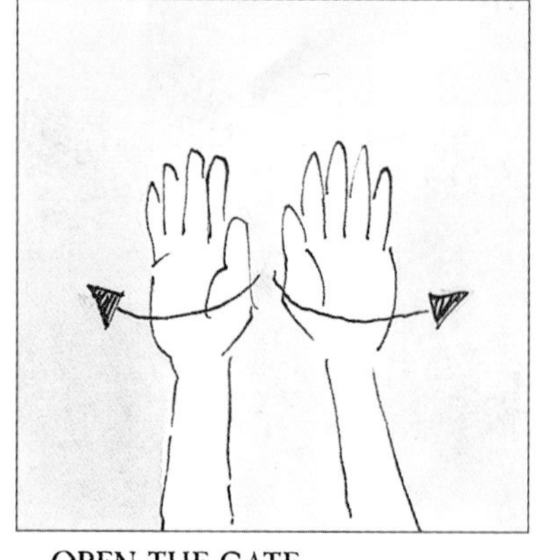

... OPEN THE GATE ...

Make fingers into ring

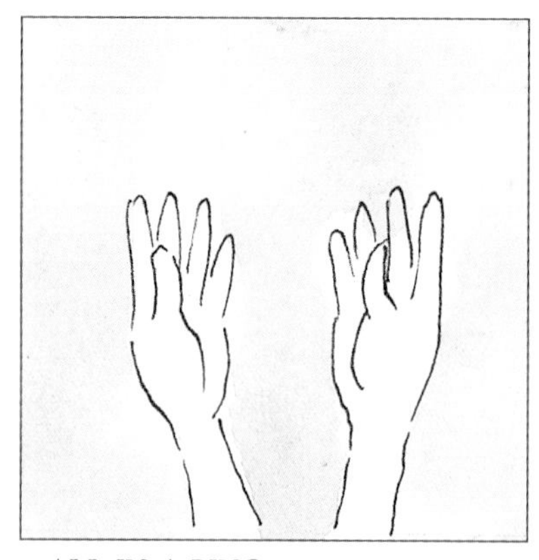

.. ALL IN A RING ...

Ten little men bow to the king,
Ten little men dance all day,
Ten little men hide away.

Bend fingers

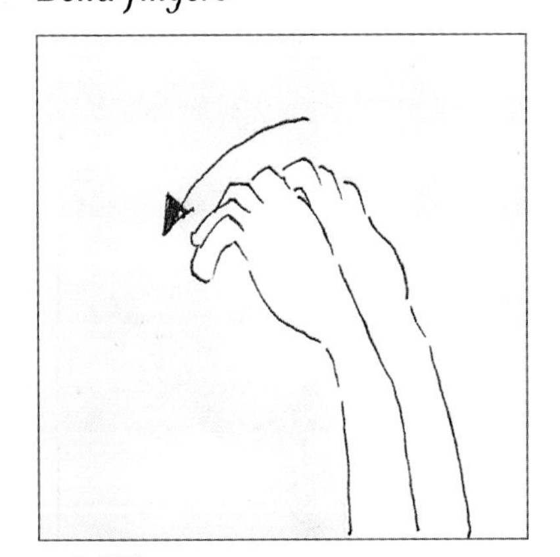

... BOW ...

Dance fingers

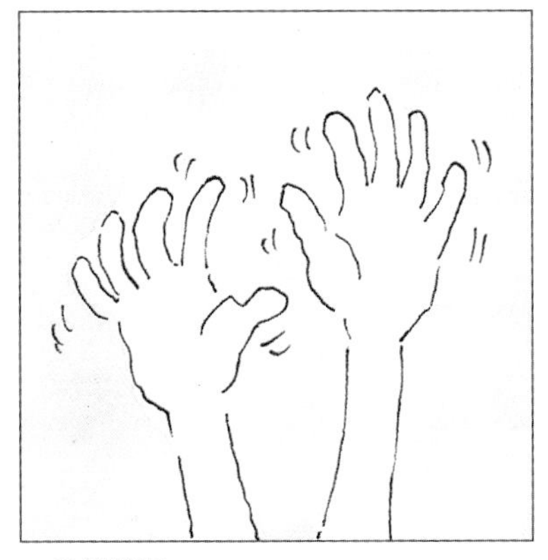

... DANCE ...

Hide hands behind back

... HIDE AWAY

Scrub Your Dirty Face

Scrub your dirty face,
Scrub your dirty face,
With a rub-a-dub-dub,
And a rub-a-dub-dub,
Scrub your dirty face.

Mime actions. Continue with hands, knees and feet

Clap Your Hands

Clap your hands, clap your hands,
Clap them just like me.
Touch your shoulders, touch your shoulders,
Touch them just like me.
Tap your knees, tap your knees,
Tap them just like me.
Shake your head, shake your head,
Shake it just like me.
Clap your hands, clap your hands,
Then let them quiet be.

I Can ...

I can tie my shoe lace,
I can brush my hair,
I can wash my hands and face
And dry myself with care.

I can clean my teeth too,
And fasten up my frocks.
I can say, "How do you do?",
And pull up both my socks.

Mime actions and put hands in lap at the end

Shoes

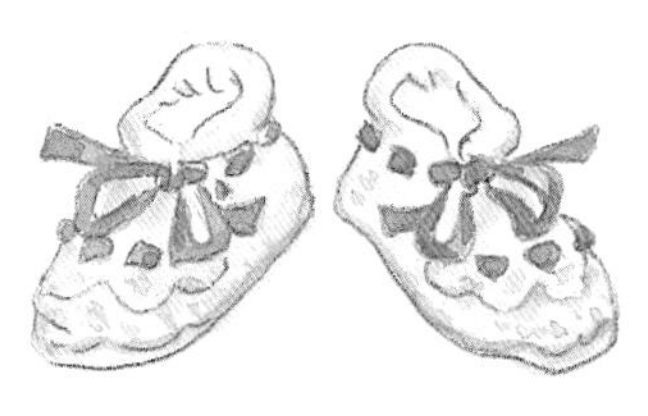

Baby's shoes,

Mother's shoes,

Father's shoes,

Policeman's shoes,

GIANT'S SHOES!

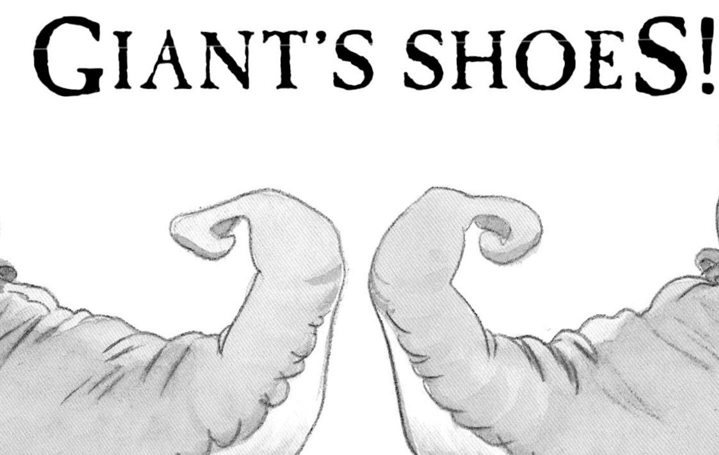

Hold hands wider apart for each pair of shoes, and make voice get louder and louder

BABY'S SHOES

MOTHER'S SHOES

FATHER'S SHOES

GIANT'S SHOES!

Dingle Dangle Scarecrow

When all the cows were sleeping
And the sun had gone to bed,
Up jumped the scarecrow
And this is what he said:

I'm a dingle dangle scarecrow
With a flippy floppy hat!
I can shake my arms like this,
I can shake my legs like that!

DINGLE DANGLE

FLIPPY FLOPPY HAT

When the cows were in the meadow
And the pigeons in the loft,
Up jumped the scarecrow
And whispered very soft:
Chorus

SHAKE MY ARMS

SHAKE MY LEGS

When all the hens were roosting
And the moon behind a cloud,
Up jumped the scarecrow
And shouted very loud:
Chorus

Peter Works with One Hammer

Peter works with one hammer,
one hammer, one hammer,
Peter works with one hammer,
this fine day.

Peter works with two hammers,
two hammers, two hammers,
Peter works with two hammers,
this fine day.

Peter works with three hammers, etc.
Peter works with four hammers, etc.
Peter works with five hammers, etc.

Bang one fist on knee in rhythm

ONE HAMMER

Bang two fists on knees

TWO HAMMERS

Bang two fists, tap one foot

THREE HAMMERS

Bang two fists, tap two feet

FOUR HAMMERS

Peter's very tired now,
tired now, tired now,
Peter's very tired now,
this fine day.

Peter's going to sleep now,
sleep now, sleep now,
Peter's going to sleep now,
this fine day.

Peter's waking up now,
up now, up now,
Peter's waking up now,
this fine day.

Bang two fists, tap two feet and nod head

FIVE HAMMERS

Rub eyes and stretch as if yawning

TIRED NOW

Pretend to sleep

GOING TO SLEEP

Pretend to wake and stretch

WAKING UP

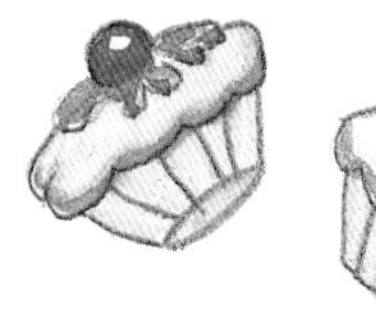 

Pat-A-Cake

Pat-a-cake, pat-a-cake,
baker's man,

Bake me a cake,
as fast as you can.

Pat it and prick it and
mark it with B,

And put it in the oven
for Baby and me.

Clap in rhythm

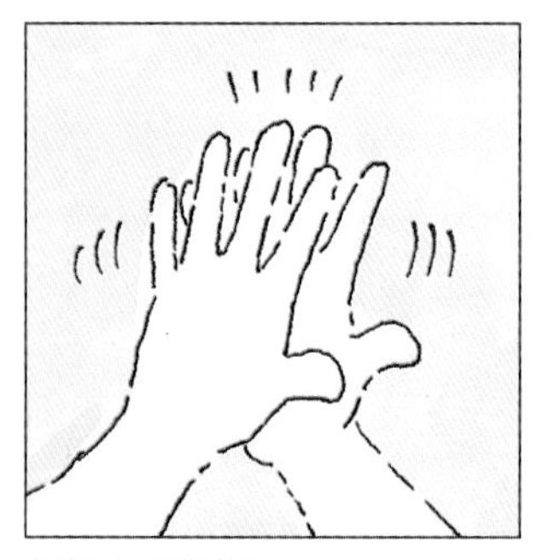

PAT-A-CAKE

Pat and 'prick' palm

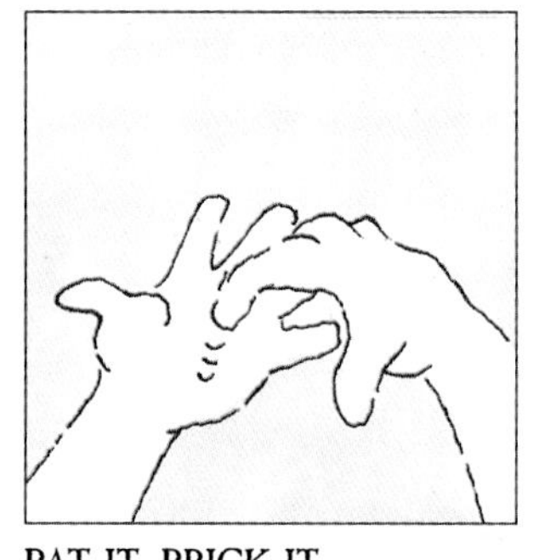

PAT IT, PRICK IT

Trace the letter B on palm

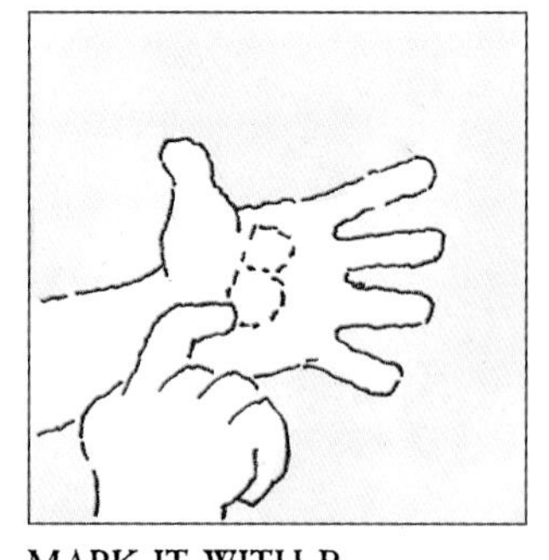

MARK IT WITH B

Put cake in oven

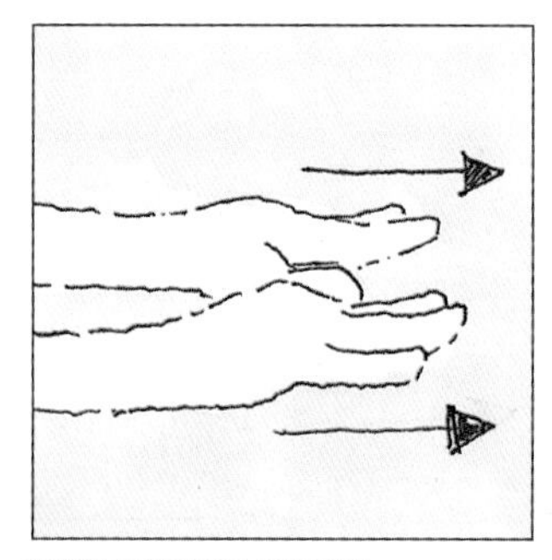

PUT IN THE OVEN

Head, Shoulders, Knees and Toes

Head, shoulders, knees
and toes, knees and toes,
Head, shoulders, knees
and toes, knees and toes,
And eyes and ears
and mouth and nose.
Head, shoulders, knees
and toes, knees and toes.

Sing slow at first, then faster.

Five Little Ducks

Five little ducks went swimming one day,
Over the hills and far away,
Mother Duck said, "Quack, quack, quack, quack,"
But only four little ducks came back.

Repeat for four, three and two little ducks...

One little duck went swimming one day,
Over the hills and far away,
Mother Duck said, "Quack, quack, quack, quack,"
And all the five little ducks came back.

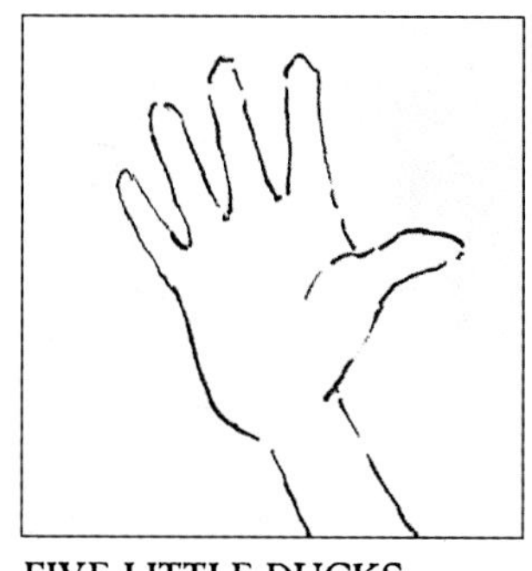

FIVE LITTLE DUCKS...

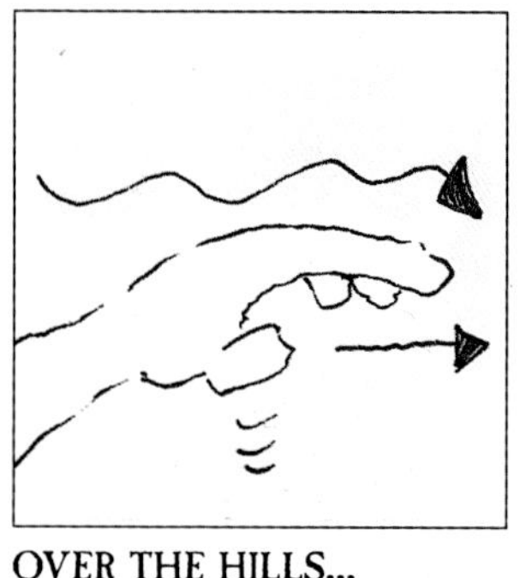

OVER THE HILLS...

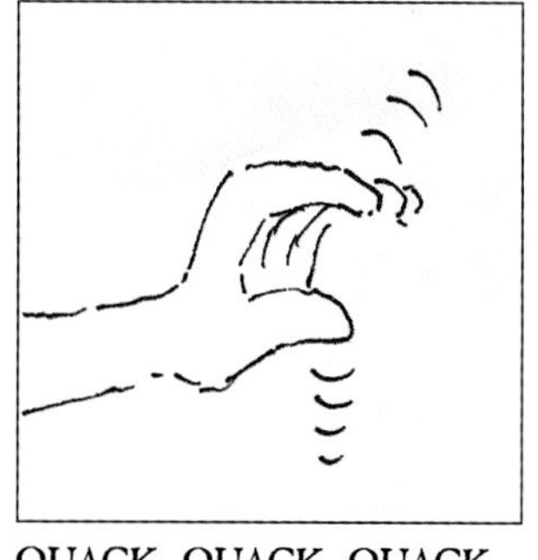

QUACK, QUACK, QUACK

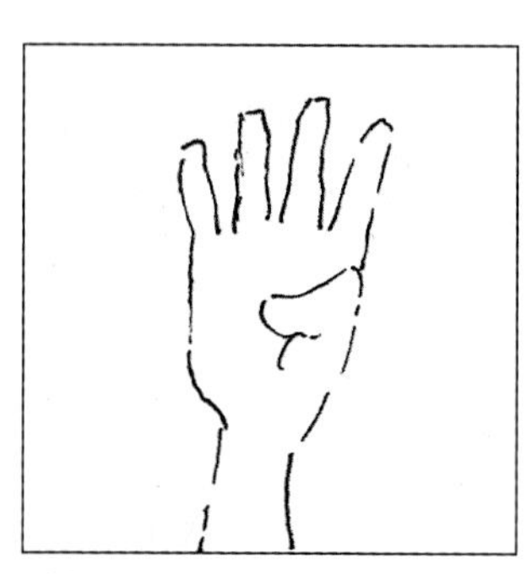

FOUR LITTLE DUCKS

See-Saw, Margery Daw
See-Saw, Margery Daw,
Johnny shall have a new master,
He shall have but a penny a day,
Because he can't work any faster.
Rock backwards and forwards

Here Is the Church

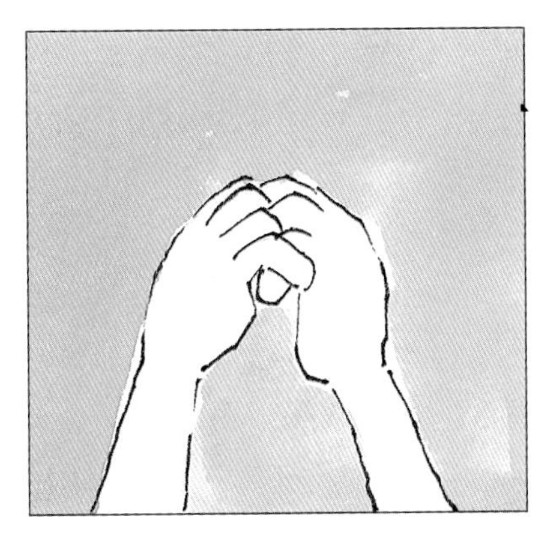

Interlace fingers

Here is the church,

Here is the steeple,

Point index fingers

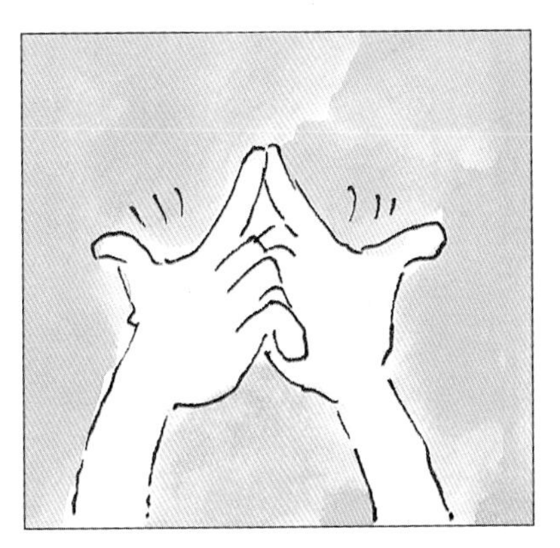

Open thumbs

Open the doors,

And here are
the people

Turn hands over and wiggle fingers

Walk fingers of one hand up fingers of other hand

Here is the parson,
going upstairs,

And here he is
a-saying his prayers

Place palms together

Tommy Thumb

Tommy Thumb,
Tommy Thumb,
Where are you?
Here I am, here I am,
How do you do?

Peter pointer, etc,
Middle Man, etc.
Ruby Ring, etc.
Baby Small, etc.

Make fists, raise thumbs and wiggle them

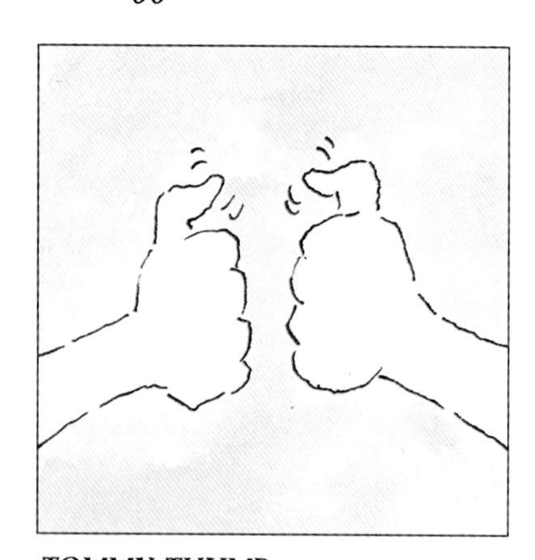

TOMMY THUMB ...

Raise forefingers and wiggle them

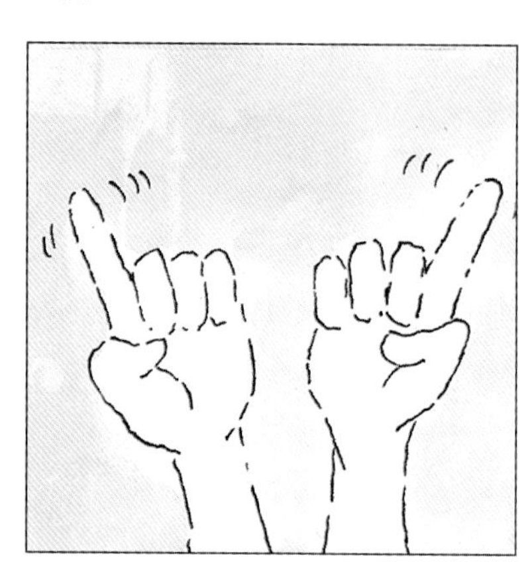

PETER POINTER ...

Raise middle fingers and wiggle them

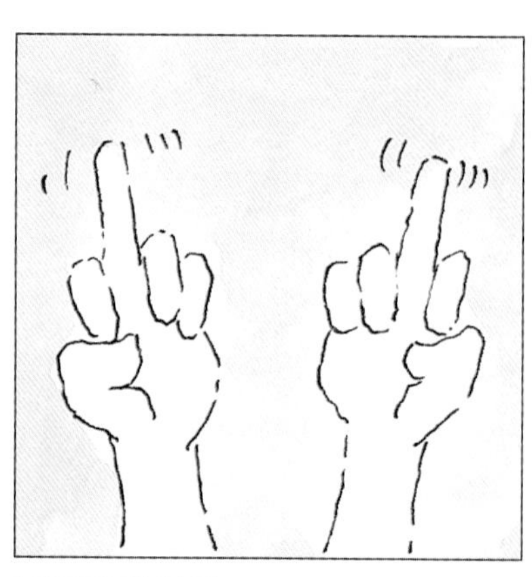

MIDDLE MAN ...

Fingers all, fingers all,
Where are you?
Here we are, here we are,
How do you do?

Raise ring fingers and wiggle them

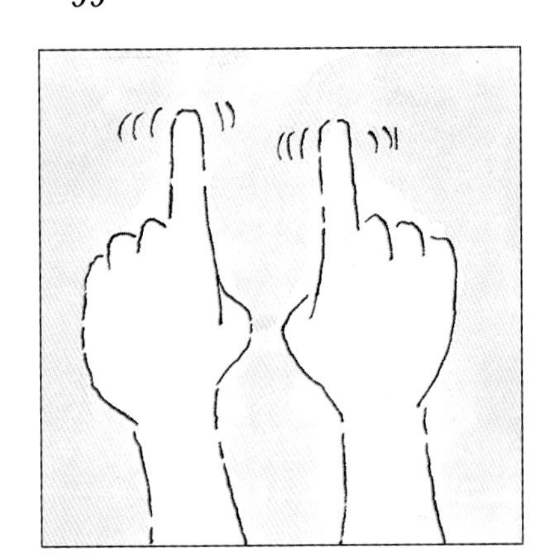

RUBY RING ...

Raise little fingers and wiggle them

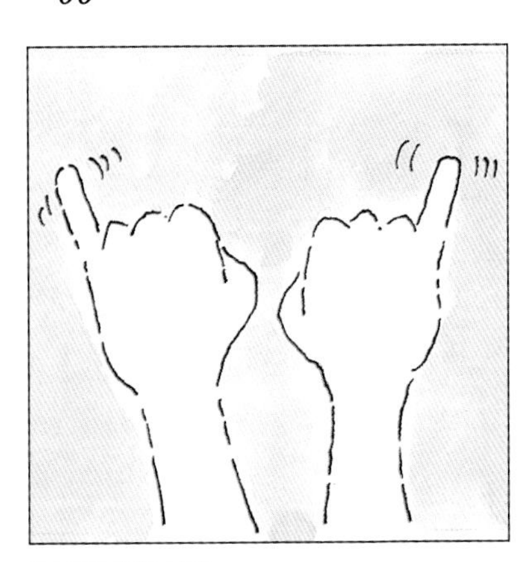

BABY SMALL ...

Raise ALL fingers and wiggle them

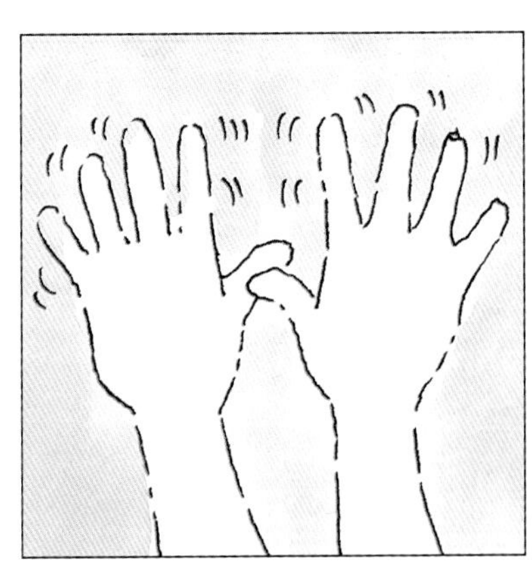

FINGERS ALL ...

The End